Throwing Back the Rope

By
Peter S. Bergeron

Throwing Back the Rope

For Caroline—

You told me, *"You won't know unless you try."*

So, I'm trying.

You told me, *"This is your match. Your move."*

So, I'm taking my shot.

And you told me, *"Win or lose, I'm in your corner."*

So, I've already won.

—Love, Peter

Table of Contents

Preface

When this began
I had nothing to say
Linkin Park – "Somewhere I belong"

The gym smelled like sweat and regret, two scents that Tyler knew far too well, even though it had been years since he last stood here. The last time he really remembered was watching the Sabers raise their first state championship banner.

Now, he lingered in the doorway, staring at the empty mat where he had once wrestled through blood, exhaustion, and anger. The banners hanging from the ceiling served as a quiet reminder of a time when the program was at its peak.

But now?

Now the Riverstone wrestling team was silent, gutted by scandal.

Hazing.

The word still hit like a gut punch every time Tyler thought about it. Riverstone wrestling had been his salvation, a place where Coach Beau's gruff voice cut through the chaos of his teenage rebellion and drove him to become tougher, sharper, and more disciplined. His bond with Johnny and

1

Robby had formed during those grueling practices, where they carried each other through Beau's relentless demands. Beau's methods often walked a fine line between tough love and brutality. Tyler carried the scars as proof.

Now, that edge had tipped, cutting deep into the heart of the program.

"They need someone to rebuild this," Principal Owens had said to Tyler just a week ago, his tone as worn as the championship banners that hung above the mat. *"They need someone who understands what this program was at its best and what it can be again."*

Tyler didn't know if he was the person for the job.

He stared at his phone, hoping for a response to the text he'd sent Robby an hour ago:

I NEED TO TALK.

It was straightforward, but it made him feel vulnerable in a way he hated. Asking for help had never come easily. Coach Beau had always warned him about that. *"You don't wrestle alone. You need to learn that, or it'll break you."*

Tyler's thoughts turned to Bryce, his son, who had led the charge to expose the hazing tactics pushed by the captains under the coaching staff's watch. The younger wrestlers, the newbies, never stood a chance. Bryce and his close friends hadn't seen what was happening at first, but when they did, they couldn't turn a blind eye.

Tyler had always been proud of that about Bryce—his unwillingness to look away when something was wrong. It was a trait that had only grown stronger over the years, maybe shaped by the divorce. Bryce had been young when he and Michelle split, but old enough to feel the shift. The back-and-forth, the tension, the quiet understanding that some things just don't work out no matter how much you want them to. Maybe that was why Bryce had become so determined to stand his ground when something needed fixing—because he knew what it felt like when things fell apart.

Bryce's decision had come at a cost.

The suspension of the entire team had cut short his junior season. Now, Bryce was saying he wouldn't wrestle his senior year.

The silence of the gym pressed in around Tyler as his eyes drifting to a faded banner from his junior year. It had been Beau's final season and would be the catalyst of a string of Riverstone titles built off the legend of the Bennett Brothers.

Tyler had been part of that story, too. He'd sacrificed for the team during both his junior and senior seasons, dropping weight to fill a critical spot and then bulking up the next summer to push Johnny Bennett toward an undefeated New England championship. Back then, Tyler had believed those sacrifices might redeem everyone he'd let down in his earlier years.

Now, they just felt like moments that had slipped away.

His phone buzzed, breaking the silence. Robby was calling.

"Let me save you some time. I already know what's going on," Robby said, his voice sharp but warm.

Tyler didn't respond immediately, still grappling with the weight of the situation. "They want me to take over the program," he finally said.

"Yeah, no shit. I called Principal Owens," Robby replied. "And Beau did too. We both told them you were the one to fix this. It's time, Tyler."

"You did what?" Tyler's voice tightened.

"Someone's gotta keep you out of the darkness," Robby said, steady but firm. "You think I forgot what you went through sophomore year? This isn't just about the team. It's about you. If Bryce doesn't go back, it's going to eat at you, and you know it. You've both had a year in the dark. It's time for you to light the way for him."

Tyler rubbed the back of his neck. "I don't even know if I can do this. You remember what it was like, Beau, the team, me screwing up."

"You think Beau didn't screw up?" Robby countered. "You're just remembering the good parts, not the time he threw his clipboard across the gym because Johnny wasn't being serious enough."

Tyler could still see the moment clearly. *Beau had been riding Johnny hard that day, just one of those "bad Beau" mood days. They were drilling different situations, and Johnny, unbothered, was singing away as he rolled around. Beau snapped and barked at him to knock off the singing.*

Without missing a beat, Johnny switched to quoting a line from Vision Quest, the cult classic wrestling movie.

"It ain't the six minutes...it's what happens in that six minutes," Johnny called out, in his best impersonation of one of the most underappreciated scenes in movie history.

The fact that the quote was Coach Beau's favorite from the movie didn't matter. Beau's clipboard flew across the mat, narrowly missing Johnny's head.

Unfazed, Johnny grinned. Robby sprang to his feet, retrieved the clipboard, and handed it back to Beau with a cheeky grin. "So, Coach, would you prefer a Spaceballs quote?"

Only Robby could have gotten away with that.

"Bryce is going to find his way," Robby said, pulling Tyler back to the present. "But he needs to see you lead first. Remember what Beau used to say, 'You don't have to be perfect. You just have to be committed to giving it your all.' That's the start, Tyler."

Tyler's eyes shifted to the banner again. "I don't want to screw this up," he admitted.

"That's why I called Owens," Robby said. "Those kids don't need perfection. They need someone who's committed to them. And so does Bryce. If not you, then who? Think about what Beau always said about Snake. Whenever Beau wanted to practice, Snake was there, he always showed up, always ready to push him, to help him get better. He taught Beau what it meant to be supported.

"Beau gave up his summer nights running open mats for any area wrestler who wanted to show up, because Snake did the same for him. That's how it works. Someone helps you, and then it's your turn to throw the rope back to help someone else along. Now it's your turn, Tyler."

Tyler ended the call, slipping the phone back into his pocket. He wasn't sure he was the person these kids needed.

But when he thought about Bryce, he saw the same hunger he'd once had, the hunger to belong, and to matter.

Robby was right. It was time to throw back the rope.

Chapter One
Tyler: Junior Year - The Wednesday Meeting

This world could be a son of a bitch
Well, look through my eyes
Shaboozey - "Last of My Kind"

The Wednesday before the first practice of the season wasn't just another meeting, it was Coach Beau's infamous "your ass is mine" meeting, designed to set the tone for the season. Under Beau, it had become a ritual, a line drawn in the sand. For the veterans, it was a blunt reminder of the expectations awaiting them. For the younger wrestlers, it was a trial by fire.

For Tyler, sitting in the back row flanked by Robby and Johnny, it was something else entirely: a moment of reckoning. The two had dragged him here, determined not to let him back out of asking for a second chance, from a coach who made it clear on day one that he didn't waste time on anyone who wasn't committed to his team.

Coach Beau stood firm at the front of the gym, his stocky 5'8" frame radiating quiet authority. Broad shoulders filled out his Riverstone Wrestling jacket, and the whistle around his neck seemed more like a badge of rank than a coaching tool. At just 160 pounds, he carried himself with the presence of someone far larger, his sharp, no-nonsense expression daring anyone to challenge his authority. At 26, he wasn't much older than the seniors seated before him, but his commanding stance left no doubt about who was in charge.

"Alright, listen up!" Beau's voice cut through the quiet murmur of conversations. The younger wrestlers froze mid-whisper, and the veterans straightened instinctively.

"You've got five days," Beau began, pacing like a caged lion. "Five days to decide if you're ready to take this seriously. Monday isn't just the start of practice; it's the start of your commitment to this team."

Tyler slouched in the back row, arms crossed, feigning indifference. He'd been through this twice before, but this time it felt different. This time, the stakes were higher.

Beau's eyes swept the room as he continued, "Listen up. These first two weeks are about one thing: proving you belong. Don't show up Monday whining about being out of shape. You had all summer. You had all Fall. If you're not ready now, you're wasting my time."

The room went silent, except for the faint hum of the fluorescent lights overhead.

"And then," Beau said, a wicked smirk creeping across his face, the same one that always came before one of his brutal conditioning sessions, "comes Hell Week. That's when we separate the wrestlers from the boys, and you learn there's no pussyfooting on this team." Bagwell and Eddie Bennett, the senior captains and the only remaining wrestlers from Coach Beau's first season, both laughed.

It had become Coach Beau's infamous catchphrase, its origins tracing back to his first week leading the program. Just 23 years old, new to Riverstone and eager to set the tone, Beau had worn a T-shirt to practice that spelled out the difference between wrestlers and everyone else. On the back, in bold, it proclaimed: **"There's no PUSSYfooting in wrestling!"** *The design made it impossible to miss the first five letters, but since the actual word wasn't a swear word, Beau shrugged off the initial warnings.*

"You know, not everyone appreciates your choice of T-shirts, Coach," the athletic director remarked, raising an eyebrow.

Beau gave a polite nod, the kind that suggested compliance without promise. But a week later, he arrived in a sweatshirt bearing the same message. The day after that, it was a long-sleeved tee. For the rest of the week, he doubled down, wearing the phrase to every practice. It wasn't just stubbornness; it was a declaration. Beau wanted his team to understand that if you are doing nothing wrong, you stand your ground.

The message was loud and clear; the days of Riverstone wrestling being measured by others' standards were over. From now on, the team would need to live up to Beau's standards.

*****

A ripple of unease moved through the younger wrestlers. The veterans, the Bennett brothers among them, remained stone-faced. They knew what Hell Week meant. Brutal conditioning, relentless drills, and a coach who refused to accept anything less than full commitment.

"It's not gonna be easy," Beau said, his voice dropping to a near growl. "But wrestling isn't easy. It's sacrifice. It's pushing yourself further than you thought you could go. And if you don't think you can handle it, don't bother showing up Monday."

Tyler caught himself nodding along, despite the nervous flutter in his stomach. He knew exactly what Hell Week would demand of him, but the thought of sitting out another season terrified him even more.

Beau stopped pacing and faced the group; his expression was hard. "This is your shot to prove you belong. No excuses. No shortcuts. You want to wear Riverstone across the front of your singlet? Then earn it."

He paused, letting the words hang in the air. Then, with a sharp glance at the younger wrestlers, he added, "And don't think this is just about you. You're part of a team now. And this team? It doesn't carry dead weight."

As the meeting broke up, the younger kids shuffled out nervously. The veterans exchanged knowing looks, while Tyler lingered near the back. Beau's speech had rattled him, not because he doubted the coach's words, but because he knew they were true.

Last year, Tyler wasn't committed to the sport, the team, or to himself. He'd show up late to practice, skipped workouts, and assumed the team needed his natural talent on the mat. Beau hadn't seen it that way.

"Talent without effort is useless," Beau had said, the words cutting sharper than any drill. Two days before the first meet of Tyler's sophomore season, Beau had cut him from the team.

This year, Tyler was determined to prove he wasn't dead weight.

Chapter Two - The Principal's Office

What if I was chosen to write the stories
Kane Brown and Blake Shelton - "Different Man"

It wasn't the hazing that brought Tyler to Principal Owens' office, it was the fallout. The previous winter, the seniors involved had been expelled, and the team was gutted. Practices were suspended, the season cut short, and rumors of lawsuits swirled like vultures over a carcass.

Tyler shifted uneasily in the chair across from Owens' desk, staring at the meticulously arranged nameplate and framed degrees on the wall. It all felt too familiar. Too much like the conversations he'd had with Beau when he was Tyler's coach, sitting across from that hard wooden desk, enduring lectures that dug at his pride.

"Why me?" Tyler asked, leaning back to put some distance between himself and the principal's steady gaze.

"Because you're Beau's guy," Owens replied simply. "And because you know how to lead in a way these kids need right now."

Tyler barked a short laugh, one that tasted more bitter than amused. "Me? Beau's guy? The one he benched, berated, and almost broke? That guy?"

Owens tilted his head slightly, unfazed. "Yeah, that guy. The one who came back stronger. Who learned from him, found Snake's wisdom through him, and then figured out what not to do. These kids don't need a drill sergeant. They need a guide."

The words cut deeper than Tyler wanted to admit. He stared out the window, watching as a few students trudged across the courtyard, their backpacks sagging with the weight of books, or maybe just life.

"I wasn't Beau's guy," Tyler said quietly, his voice trailing off. "Not for a long time."

Owens didn't press him, letting the silence stretch between them. Tyler thought back to sophomore year, the year it all fell apart. Beau's hard-nosed coaching had clashed with the growing anger Tyler couldn't put into words back then. He'd been stubborn, self-absorbed, and so sure he didn't need anyone. Beau's way of breaking down wrestlers to build them back up felt like an attack on Tyler's independence, and he fought back the only way he knew how, by pushing away.

Sophomore year had been a blur of excuses and resentment. Tyler skipped practices, half-assed workouts, and eventually, Beau told him to stop coming altogether. In that moment, Beau made the decision Tyler couldn't admit he'd already made; he was done with Riverstone Wrestling.

It wasn't until junior year, after an offhand comment from Robby, that Tyler found himself back in the gym that Wednesday before the first practice. Robby and Johnny had been there when Tyler was at his lowest, so he couldn't turn his back on them.

"You can't battle through this alone, Ty," Johnny had told him the summer before junior year. He'd adapted it from one of Beau's mantras: *You don't wrestle alone.* Beau drilled it into his wrestlers—look to the corner, lean on those around you. They help you through the match. Your partners push you further.

Tyler had come back to the team that year, with hat in hand, and a fire he hadn't felt before. But the scars from that year of self-imposed exile were still there. And now Owens was sitting here, asking him to take over a program that had been dragged through the mud and left to rot.

Tyler shook his head, exhaling sharply. "Bryce is not going to wrestle. And me coaching is most likely going to seal the deal on that."

Owens raised an eyebrow, leaning forward. "Why?"

"Because he's still pissed. About last year. About the team. About me." Tyler's voice faltered as he admitted it, the words hanging in the air like an accusation he couldn't dodge. "He thinks I let him down by not fighting enough for him with the school board. Hell, maybe I did."

Owens didn't respond right away. He folded his hands on the desk, his expression unreadable. "Bryce has every right to be angry. What happened last year was... a failure on many levels. But you stepping into this role doesn't have to be about Bryce. It has to be about rebuilding something bigger than both of you."

14

Tyler laughed again, though this time it came out softer. "You've got a lot of faith in me, Owens."

"You're not perfect, Tyler. Neither was Beau. But he was exactly what this program needed back then, and now it needs you."

The words landed harder than Tyler expected. Owens wasn't wrong. Beau's tough-love approach had shaped him, but it had also left cracks Tyler spent years repairing. He wasn't Beau. He didn't want to be.

"Alright," Tyler said finally, his voice steady. "But I'm doing it my way."

Owens smiled faintly. "Good. That's what these kids need."

As Tyler left Owens' office, his mind churned. He wanted to believe Owens was right, but the weight of Bryce's anger, and his own doubts, pressed heavily on his chest. He thought about the scars Beau had left on him, the lessons he'd struggled to make sense of, and whether he could lead without repeating the same mistakes.

Doing it his way was the promise he'd made, but now he had to figure out exactly what that meant. And fast.

Chapter Three — Tyler: last day of 8ᵗʰ grade

We grew up way too fast
And now there's nothing to believe
Goo Goo Dolls – "Name"

The last day of eighth grade was supposed to be simple, a half-day of classes, signing yearbooks, and the start of summer. But for Tyler, it marked the end of everything he thought he understood about the world.

The family barbecue that evening was loud and chaotic, as always. Cousins darted around the yard, uncles traded bad jokes, and the smoky scent of burgers wafted from the grill. Tyler had wandered inside, hoping to catch a bit of the Red Sox game before anyone noticed he was gone. That's when he heard the muffled sobs.

It wasn't unusual for Jacob to disappear during family events. Over the years, he had grown more withdrawn, quiet, shy even. But this was different. The sound made Tyler stop in his tracks. He hesitated outside the guest room, unsure whether to knock or walk away. Then, through the thin crack of the door, he saw it.

Jacob's stepdad. Jacob.

The moment hit Tyler like a punch to the chest. He jumped away from the door before his presence was noticed and stumbled into the hallway, his breaths coming in short gasps. His hands trembled as he gripped the wall for support.

His mind screamed at him to do something, anything, but his body refused to move.

The rest of the evening passed in a blur. Tyler avoided Jacob, avoided Jacob's stepdad, avoided everyone. He felt trapped, like he was carrying a secret too heavy to bear but too terrifying to speak aloud.

At home that night, Tyler sat on the edge of his bed, staring at the carpet. His mom knocked softly before stepping inside.

"Tyler? You've been quiet all night. What's going on?" Her voice was gentle, but her eyes searched his face with concern.

He couldn't look at her. "Nothing. I'm fine," he muttered.

*****

But Tyler wasn't fine. Over the next weeks, his fire for wrestling dimmed. He stopped running in the mornings, skipped lifting sessions, and ignored Beau's calls asking why he wasn't showing up to open mat nights. The sound of Jacob's sobs haunted him, gnawing at his sense of control.

The truth finally broke loose late one night when his mom found him sitting alone on the porch steps, his head in his hands.

"I can't," he whispered when she asked what was wrong.

"You can't what?" she pressed, kneeling beside him.

He looked at her then, his face streaked with tears. "I can't keep it in anymore. It's Jacob. His stepdad..."

The words came out in choked sobs, but his mom didn't flinch. She listened, her face a mix of shock and quiet determination.

"We're going to help him," she said firmly. "You don't have to carry this alone."

Her words should have been comforting, but instead, Tyler felt the weight of what was to come. He wanted to help Jacob, but he couldn't shake the fear of what speaking out would unleash.

A few months later, Tyler's mom stayed behind to talk to Coach Beau after an informational night for the team parents. The session had featured a segment on nutrition. While Beau demanded his wrestlers push themselves to the limits of what their bodies could handle, he wanted parents to be properly informed on how to keep their kids eating healthy, even on an ultra-low-calorie diet. The parents saw it as a young coach concerned for his wrestlers' health. In reality, it was Beau's way of preempting complaints when the kids inevitably whined about being starved.

"When your wrestler comes home from practice, finishes their salad with a little bit of tuna fish on it, a drizzle of oil and vinegar—no dressing," the young, attractive nutritionist said with a practiced smile, "and then starts complaining they're starving and need dessert, hand them a rice cake. It's an excellent, healthy snack for a wrestler who needs to keep the calories low."

The parents chuckled, some exchanging knowing looks. One of the dads muttered, "Good luck with that," earning a wave of laughter from the group.

Beau stood off to the side, arms crossed, his expression a mix of approval and amusement. He caught the nutritionist's eye and gave her a quick wink, followed by a grin that walked the line between charming and mischievous. The nutritionist rolled her eyes with a smirk but didn't miss a beat as she continued.

As the parents filtered out, Tyler's mom lingered, waiting until the room was nearly empty. She approached Beau, hesitating only briefly.

"Coach, I think you should know," she started, her voice low but steady. "Tyler's been struggling. Really struggling."

Beau turned to face her fully, his sharp eyes softening. "Go on," he said.

Chapter Four — New Coach

Life around me's changing too fast
And you can't replace what's stuck in the past
Bailey Zimmerman – "Pain Won't Last"

"What the hell was that? 'I'm doing it my way'?
Fucking dumbass." Bryce heard his dad muttering from the
office as he reached the top of the stairs. His dad talked to
himself a lot, so it wasn't surprising to hear a one-sided
conversation. Lately though, it felt like all their interactions
were one-sided, more like lectures than conversations, the
kind you get when you're trapped in the passenger seat after
a tournament.

Bryce kept walking toward his room, hoping to avoid
another one of those "talks."

"Bryce, hey," his dad called from the office, the tone
more deliberate than usual. "I need to talk to you about
something."

Bryce sighed, pausing in the hallway. "Sure, what's up,
Dad?" He leaned against the doorframe, arms crossed,
already hoping this wouldn't take long.

Tyler leaned back in his chair; his posture unusually
serious. "It's about your new head coach."

"Head coach of what, Dad?"

"Wrestling. Your wrestling team, Bryce. Come on,
what other team would I be talking about?"

Bryce straightened, the annoyance creeping into his voice. "I'm done, Dad. I don't care who they bring in; I'm done. The coaches last year knew what was going on. They did nothing. Our season got screwed because of their inaction, and then those of us who did the right thing got punished the same as the assholes who caused it. I'm done with that team."

Tyler raised an eyebrow, his tone calm but pointed. "Well, that sucks. I was looking forward to coaching you this year. It's been awhile."

That made Bryce pause. "You're coaching? High school?"

"Yeah. And it would really help to have at least one person I know will actually listen."

Bryce let out a dry laugh. "For you, I'll think about it. But no promises I'll listen. Oh, and don't forget, the weight classes and some other rules have changed since your days on the mat, so you might want to do some studying too."

He smirked, and Tyler shook his head, a small smile tugging at his lips. For a second, Bryce saw something in his dad's expression, a flicker of Coach Beau, the legendary hard-ass Tyler had learned from. It made Bryce uneasy and oddly proud at the same time.

*****

Bryce headed to his room, shutting the door behind him. He sank onto his bed, staring at the ceiling. There was a time when wrestling had been everything. He could still feel the sting of last season, the weight of knowing he'd done the right thing, even as it cost the team their shot at a championship. The memory clawed its way back.

Nick hunched over in the locker room, eyes red, and glassy, trying to pull himself together. The quiet tension in the air when Bryce and the others walked in. The sick, heavy knowledge of what had just happened and the unspoken agreement not to talk about it.

But Bryce couldn't ignore it, not after seeing the look in Nick's eyes. It wasn't fear; it was worse. It was defeat. That was the moment Bryce knew he couldn't stay silent.

He remembered the conversation under the bleachers with Johnson, the only other wrestler he trusted enough to talk about what they'd seen. The air was heavy, stifling, even outside. Bryce's pulse pounded in his ears, his fists clenching and unclenching at his sides.

"We have to go to Owens," Bryce said, his voice low but firm.

Johnson shook his head, glancing over his shoulder as if someone might be listening. "If we go to Owens, you know what happens. They shut us down. Season over."

Bryce stepped closer; his jaw was tight. "So, we just let this slide? Let Nick deal with this alone?"

Johnson didn't answer, but the guilt in his eyes said enough.

Bryce pressed on. "Look, I get it. It sucks. But we're supposed to be leaders, right? Leaders set the standard. This isn't it."

He had given up a lot for wrestling, more than most people realized. When his mom left for Georgia, he could've gone with her. She had a good job lined up, a fresh start, but the high school there didn't have wrestling. That had been a dealbreaker. So, he stayed. He stayed with his dad, with the team, with the only thing that felt solid when everything else was breaking apart.

Now, looking at Johnson, he felt that same weight again—that same choice. Walk away and protect himself, or stand his ground and fight for what mattered?

For Bryce, there was never really a choice. Johnson exhaled, rubbing the back of his neck. "You know they'll hate us for it."

Bryce shrugged, the weight of his decision already settling on his shoulders. "I'll hate myself more if we do nothing. Don't worry, I'll take the heat."

And he did. Bryce was the one who went to Owens. He was the one who stood in the principal's office, recounting everything he knew. He was the one who watched the

23

captains get expelled, the season got canceled, and the entire team collapsed under the weight of a scandal no one wanted to deal with.

Bryce clenched his jaw, staring at the ceiling. Wrestling had once been everything, a place where he'd found purpose and pride. Now, it felt like a broken promise, one he wasn't sure he could trust again. He grabbed his phone and sent a quick text to Johnson: **"HEY, NEED TO TALK."**

Chapter Five — Tyler: Junior Year — Coach Beau's Office

It's not a question, but a lesson learned in time
Green Day - "Good Riddance"

Beau wasn't thrilled with what he was seeing. Tyler sat slumped in the hard, wooden chair across from Beau's desk, his posture all but crumbling under the weight of the silence. The fear in Tyler's eyes told Beau he needed to start this conversation or they would be stuck in this standoff all day.

"You think you deserve to be back on this team?" Beau's voice emphasized the word *deserve*, slicing through the air. This was what had pushed Beau over the edge last season, Tyler's sense of entitlement about being part of the team. Beau and Tyler's mom had talked about it often. Beau had been adamant that Tyler needed to understand he needed wrestling, and the team, not the other way around. Until Tyler could see that he had to lean on others and stop trying to tackle his obstacles alone, he would only sink deeper into the darkness. Sometimes, you needed to shut the light off to force someone to fight to find it again.

The two of them had been working behind the scenes to guide Tyler. Beau was an unlikely confidant, but he seemed to understand Tyler in ways his mom couldn't. Maybe it was because Beau carried his own shadows, an understanding of what it meant to feel like you'd failed to protect, to lead, to save others from slipping into the dark. It wasn't just something he saw in Tyler; it was something he recognized from his own past.

For Beau, those moments had shaped him, and he had spent years learning to channel them into something better, something that could help others. He saw those same flickers in Tyler now: the fear, the doubt, and the temptation to pull back instead of leaning on others. Beau knew what it was like to walk that edge, and if he could help Tyler find a way forward, maybe he could keep him from making the same missteps. He wasn't just guiding Tyler for Tyler's sake. In some ways, he was still fighting his own battle, helping Tyler to hold on to the light before it slipped too far out of reach.

Tyler swallowed hard. "I messed up. I know that. But I'll do whatever it takes, Coach. I just need another chance."

Beau leaned back, folding his arms across his chest. "Whatever it takes, huh? Let me tell you something, Tyler. Being on this team isn't a right. It's a privilege. And privileges come with sacrifices. Are you ready for that?"

"I am, Coach." Beau could see the fear in Tyler's eyes, but not the confidence he had hoped for. It was the same hesitation Beau had been bracing himself to see. He needed to push harder, to get Tyler to react.

"How about the nonsense from freshman and sophomore year? The immature kid who didn't show anyone respect, is that behind you?" Beau snapped.

"Coach, last season sitting on the outside looking in, being locked out from getting under that light, not having a chance to be out there competing—it sucked." Beau finally saw a flicker of fire in Tyler's eyes. There it was. *Hunger.*

"And sacrifice?"

"Again, whatever it takes."

A small grin crossed Beau's face. This was what he wanted to see: hunger, desperation, a need to be part of the program.

"Even if it means dropping close to 15 pounds? Because the only spot open is at 130. Unless you are planning on bulking up over Thanksgiving break to take on Campbell at 160. But let's be honest, you are not quite ready to move out of lane two." Beau was referring to one of his favorite drills, a concept from his Salem High wrestling days called "Lover's Lane." It was a gauntlet where newer wrestlers and backups rotated through starters, each facing different positions: neutral, top, or bottom. It was a battle of will for the backups and a test of heart for the starters. The 160-weight class bridged lane two, the middleweights, and lane three, the upperweights. Tyler had spent too much time in lane two and knew Beau was right. He wasn't ready for 160.

"130?" The fear crept back into Tyler's face, but Beau had him hooked. It was time to lay out the reality. This was the only rope Tyler could climb to get out of the darkness.

"Bagwell's at 135. Eddie's at 145. Both captains. You know the rules. Captains name their spots, and everyone else falls in line. You could challenge Johnny at 140, but that is your call. Tommy is holding down 152."

Tyler shook his head. Johnny, the middle Bennett brother, was the best technician on the team. Tommy, the youngest, was easily the strongest. Tyler knew he had no chance against either of them. He had tossed Bagwell around as a freshman, but Bagwell had since transformed into a disciplined machine, while Tyler had been "uninvited" from the team for his sophomore year. But it didn't matter, Bagwell was a captain.

Beau leaned forward; his voice sharp but not unkind. "Listen, don't decide now. Take the next few days to think about it. Once you make your decision, you own it, Tyler. But before you commit, talk to your mom. She needs to be on board because this won't just be tough on you. It will be a sacrifice you can't face alone."

With that, Beau dismissed him.

*****

"FUCK...I blew it," Tyler muttered under his breath, walking out of the locker room.

"Well, what did he say?" Robby asked, sitting on a bench with Johnny.

Tyler hesitated. "I think I blew it."

"What the hell, Ty? You had one job!" Robby threw his arms up in frustration. Tyler couldn't help but notice how much Robby mimicked Beau's mannerisms.

"What do you mean?" Johnny asked calmly. Johnny was the rock of the team, the one who never flinched when Beau's wrath came down.

"Beau said if I want a varsity spot, it's at 130."

"Okay, so what's the problem?"

"I hesitated! I didn't say yes right away."

Robby groaned. "Ty, he asked all of us the same thing today. He's testing everyone. This season's going to be brutal, he's pushing us to be state champs. You've got time to figure it out, but don't screw around."

"Ty, seriously, what's holding you back?" Johnny pressed.

"I don't know if I can do it," Tyler admitted. "I'm not worried about the physical part, I mean, it's going to suck, but I can handle that. It's the mental grind."

Johnny nodded. "Yeah, it's going to be tough, but we'll get through it."

"We?" Tyler asked.

"Yeah," Johnny said, giving him a "duh" look. "You think we'd let you do this alone?"

"I get it, but it's dropping close to 15 pounds. What the hell are you guys going to do to make that happen?" Tyler's voice carried more frustration than he intended.

"When are you going to cut that shit out?" Robby snapped. "You pulled this at the courthouse, you're pulling it now. It's getting old."

Johnny cut in; his tone gentler. "What Robby's saying, without any sense of feeling, is that we're in this together. This is our team, Ty. Sure, Eddie and Bagwell are the captains, but we're the ones who kept this program alive. We've faced everything Beau's thrown at us before, and we'll handle this too."

Robby nodded. "I've done a bigger cut than what you're looking at, and trust me, I wasn't exactly a lean machine back then. Remember when Beau took me to Shaw's and showed me how to eat right? You can do it too."

Tyler exhaled. He didn't need to make the decision yet, but he could feel the weight of it pressing on him.

"Beau said I need to clear it with my mom first."

Johnny smirked. "Oh, yeah, you're on your own for that one. Let's go get some Rice Cakes, though."

"They any good?" Tyler asked, feigning optimism.

"Ever tasted Styrofoam? Pretty much sums them up," Robby quipped.

"Sounds awesome. 130—this is gonna suck." Tyler laughed, finally feeling a small spark of determination as they walked out of the high school lobby.

Chapter Six – Tyler: Summer before Junior Year

I feel it in the air
The summer's out of reach
Don Henley – "The Boys of Summer"

"Michael Beaudet, how can I help you?" Beau tried using his most professional tone whenever answering his work phone. In reality, he was actively trying to master computer solitaire to survive another thrilling day as a disability insurance brokerage representative. His job mostly involved writing quotes for people who had a skill he didn't: closing sales. Beau had taken the job for the freedom to coach—he had no interest in being an insurance agent, and his sales performance made that clear. So, the company moved him from sales to support. Which meant unlimited solitaire.

"Hi, Coach. I'm sorry to bother you at work, but the trial starts on Monday, and..." Tyler's mom paused. "He's shutting everyone out, Coach. I'm scared. You said it—we can't have him face this alone."

"He won't." Beau's response was short, direct, and filled with purpose.

"But he won't talk to anyone."

"He won't be alone. I've got it. You just get him there and remind him he's not alone. You focus on you, and I'll take care of this." That was Beau's way. He didn't ask for permission to help; he simply told you he would, reminding you that you didn't need to carry the darkness alone. Beau would shoulder it for you.

After hanging up, Beau opened an email to Adam Bennett, the Bennett brothers' dad and the unofficial big brother figure in his life. Adam wasn't just the team's biggest supporter; he was the one who held Beau accountable when his antics became too childish.

Subject: *Dinner and convo I need to have with Johnny and Robby.*

*****

A few hours later, Beau sat at the picnic table in the Bennetts' backyard. The crackle of high-voltage power lines a few hundred yards away was the only sound breaking the quiet of a warm New Hampshire summer night. Robby and Johnny sat across from him, still sweaty from the open mat session Beau had run earlier, their dinner courtesy of the Bennett parents, the real saviors of the Riverstone program.

Adam hadn't known much about wrestling when Eddie first fell in love with the sport, but he'd been hooked ever since. He supported the team with everything he had, and in turn, he supported Beau, even when Beau's methods needed reining in.

"Boys," Beau began, his voice unusually serious, "I need to tell you some things about what's really been happening with Tyler. A lot of this, he's been too ashamed to share, but he's got nothing to be ashamed of. This isn't going to be a normal conversation coming from me, but you two need to understand what Tyler is going through and what you need to do to help him from drifting too far off course."

And with that, Beau told them what he'd hoped he wouldn't have to. He shared the details Tyler couldn't, putting into words the darkness Tyler was battling. Beau didn't like shining a light on someone else's struggles, but in this moment to help Tyler, he had to. He understood how to translate that kind of darkness better than most, a gift Beau hadn't learned, but one he carried like a weight.

*****

The trial had been scheduled for months. Tyler had known it was coming, but that didn't make the summons any easier. The weight of it all felt unbearable: the questions, the courtroom, the pressure of standing in front of strangers and exposing what he'd seen.

He sat in the back of his mom's car on the way to court, staring at his hands. They hadn't stopped shaking since he woke up.

"You don't have to do this alone," his mom said, glancing at him in the rearview mirror.

Her words echoed what she'd said months ago, but they didn't make him feel any better, yet less alone.

When they arrived, the courthouse was cold and sterile, its walls heavy with quiet dread. Tyler spotted Jacob and his mom sitting in the lobby, their faces pale and drawn.

Tyler wasn't sure how long he'd been sitting there when he heard someone call his name. He looked up to see Robby and Johnny standing in the hallway, their expressions steady and resolute.

"Coach told us what's going on," Robby said, clapping a hand on Tyler's shoulder. "We're here for you."

Tyler blinked, unsure of what to say. The weight of the moment pressed heavily on his chest, yet their presence felt like a lifeline.

"No, you two should go. You don't want to be here; I don't want you here. Please, just go," Tyler protested, his voice wavering. He couldn't be seen as weak around Johnny and Robby. He had already pulled away from them. He didn't want them to hear what he had to say. Shame anchored his words.

"Listen, we're here for you. We get it. Don't worry, we've got your back," Robby said, flashing his goofy grin.

"I didn't ask you to have my back, Robby. Seriously, I don't need you." Tyler's tone was sharper than intended, but he couldn't bring himself to soften it.

"Tyler," Johnny said calmly, his steady voice cutting through the tension. "I get it. I won't pretend to understand what you're feeling right now—it's heavier than anything I'd want to handle. But you're doing the right thing. You're helping your cousin, and that's what matters. And we're here for you because that's what teammates do. It's what friends do."

Tyler clenched his jaw, feeling the warmth of their words against the cold wall of his defenses. Begrudgingly, he accepted their support, and the three of them walked into the courtroom together.

Inside, the courtroom was colder than the lobby. The eyes of the judge and lawyers felt like daggers. Tyler's throat tightened as he took the stand. His hands gripped the edges of the chair, his pulse roaring in his ears.

"Tell us what you saw," the prosecutor said, his voice calm but firm.

Tyler hesitated, his mind racing with fear and doubt. But then he glanced at the gallery. Robby and Johnny sat behind his mom, their presence like a wall of quiet support.

Tyler took a deep breath. "I walked into the room, and I saw..." His voice shook as he recounted the events, but he didn't stop. For Jacob, he couldn't stop.

When it was over, Tyler walked out of the courthouse with Robby and Johnny flanking him. He didn't say anything, but Robby's hand stayed on his shoulder, steadying him.

"You did it," Johnny said simply.

Tyler wasn't sure he believed him, but for the first time in years, the weight on his chest felt a little lighter.

Chapter Seven — First Practice as Coach

Think I need a devil to help me get things right
Hook me up a new revolution
Foo Fighters – "Learn to Fly"

The sounds that greeted Tyler as he entered the gym were like the Sirens' song, irresistibly calling him home, the squeak of wrestling shoes on the floor blending with the steady rhythm of warm-up laps. Tyler stood by the door, clipboard in hand, trying to channel an aura of authority he didn't yet feel. He'd spent the last few nights planning this moment, combing through Coach Beau's old playbooks and his own memories. Now, he was standing in front of the Riverstone wrestling team, a group that looked more like a loose collection of individuals than a cohesive unit.

"Bring it in," Coach Tyler yelled out. The team slowly clustered around the edge of the mat. The veterans grouped on one side, their faces hard with skepticism. Bryce leaned against the gym wall, arms crossed, wearing an expression Tyler couldn't quite decipher. The younger wrestlers huddled on the other side, glancing nervously between Bryce and Tyler, waiting to see who they should follow.

Tyler cleared his throat, and the conversations quieted. He walked to the center of the mat, feeling the weight of every eye on him. "Alright, listen up," he started, his voice steady but strained. "We've got work to do. A lot of it."

The silence was heavy, expectant. He took a breath and pressed on. "Wrestling is hard. You all know that, and you accept that, or you wouldn't be here. But surviving this sport? That's something else. You can't do it alone. You need each other. You need me. And , I need you to actually listen."

A couple of younger wrestlers exchanged quick glances, while the veterans remained impassive. Bryce didn't move; his expression unchanged.

Tyler stepped closer to the group, letting his voice deepen. "This program? It used to mean something. State championships. Banners. We had a legacy, and somewhere along the way, we lost it. But legacies aren't built overnight. They're built in rooms like this, on mats like this, with teams like this."

A faint rustle of movement caught his attention. A freshman shifted his weight, his eyes flickering with a spark of interest. Tyler latched onto that flicker, letting it guide him. "This isn't about me. It's about you. What kind of team do you want to be? What kind of legacy do you want to leave behind?"

Bryce scoffed softly, just loud enough to be heard. Tyler's gaze snapped to him. "Got something to add, Bryce?"

Bryce straightened, shrugging with exaggerated indifference. "Just wondering if all this talk means we're not actually gonna wrestle and practice today is just a motivational seminar."

A ripple of laughter ran through the veterans. Tyler didn't flinch. Instead, he met Bryce's eyes head-on. "Good point. Let's wrestle."

*****

The practice started with drills, simple and familiar. Tyler moved among the pairs, correcting stances and offering pointers. His words were met with nods from the younger wrestlers and stony silence from the veterans. Bryce paired with another senior, dominating the drills with effortless precision.

As the session wore on, Tyler called for takedown sparring. Bryce and his partner squared off, their movements sharp and aggressive. Tyler watched closely, noting the way Bryce toyed with his opponent before driving him to the mat with a thud. It was impressive, but it wasn't helping his partner improve.

"Hold up," Tyler called, stepping onto the mat. He tapped Bryce's opponent on the shoulder and said, "Switch with me."

The gym fell silent as Bryce hesitated. Tyler dropped his whistle and stepped forward. "You want to prove you're too good for this team? Let's see it."

Bryce smirked and took his place in the circle. The room tightened around them, the team forming an unspoken ring as Tyler crouched into position. The whistle blew, and

Bryce shot forward. Tyler braced, countering with a sprawl that sent Bryce skidding off balance. The room erupted in murmurs.

Bryce came again; more calculated this time. Tyler matched him move for move, his body remembering instincts honed years ago. They grappled, intensity building, until Bryce managed a sweep that brought Tyler to his knees. Tyler grunted but recovered quickly, twisting out of Bryce's grip. He pinched Bryce's right shoulder with his left arm while driving Bryce's head down with his right hand, slowly pushing his hips away. Then, Tyler eased the pressure on Bryce's head, creating the illusion of freedom and prompting Bryce to lift his head and look to the sky. In an instant, Tyler corkscrewed his right hip to the mat and used his right arm to catch Bryce's head and shoulder. Bryce's right shoulder twisted further down until, suddenly... PANCAKE. Bryce flipped onto his back. It was Coach Beau's favorite counter to an overly aggressive opponent, always using the momentum of the other person against them.

Bryce tried to bridge, lifting his shoulders off the mat, but Tyler had finished the move with a headlock. Bryce finally laid flat on the mat in defeat. Tyler stood, extending his hand to Bryce. "You've got talent," he said, loud enough for the team to hear. "But talent without discipline? It's just wasted potential."

Bryce stared at him for a moment before taking the hand. Tyler helped him up, clapping him on the shoulder. *"You're better than this,"* he said quietly. *"Start showing it."*

The practice ended with conditioning drills. Tyler pushed the team hard, channeling a little bit of Coach Beau's Hell Week mentality. As the wrestlers sprawled on the mat, drenched in sweat, Tyler addressed them one last time.

"Today was just the beginning," he said. "We've got a long way to go, but I saw something out there. Keep showing me that, and we'll build something worth remembering."

As the team filed out, Tyler caught a glimpse of Bryce lingering by the door. Their eyes met, and for the first time, Bryce didn't look defiant.

In that moment, Bryce showed there was a little bit of hope.

Chapter Eight – Tyler: Junior Year – First Practice

You know where you are?

You're in the jungle baby

You're gonna die

Guns N' Roses – "Welcome to the Jungle"

Wrestling sneakers echoed through the Riverstone gym as Tyler pushed open the heavy double doors. Younger wrestlers struggled to set up the mats for practice, their movements hurried and awkward. The familiar smell of sweat and liniment hit him like a wave, stirring a mix of nostalgia and anxiety. As the mats unrolled, the stark black circle with the roaring Saber logo came into view. Tyler couldn't help but think it resembled Coach Beau yelling from the corner. He chuckled under his breath. *"Probably smart not to share that one today,"* he whispered as he stepped to the edge of the mat.

The veterans were scattered across the gym, stretching and murmuring in low voices. Johnny and Eddie Bennett, their physiques honed from years of dominance on the mat, barely acknowledged him. They were too focused on a bit of brotherly sparring, the casts on their forearms wrapped in bubble wrap.

A few weeks earlier, Coach Beau convinced a head official at a pre-season tournament to let Eddie compete with his cast wrapped. Forced to adapt, Eddie turned into a sweep single machine, relying on precision and grit to dominate. In the finals, he secured a hard-fought victory, but it wasn't without controversy.

As Eddie celebrated, the father of his opponent charged down from the stands, his face red with anger. "Your wrestler toyed with my son!" he shouted, jabbing a finger in Beau's direction. *"Letting him up over and over—what kind of coach lets that happen? That's cocky bullshit, not wrestling!"*

Beau took a step forward, meeting the man's aggression head-on. *"You want to talk about bullshit? My wrestler's got one goddamn arm!"* he snapped, his voice booming across the gym. *"We weren't about to keep him on top running moves with a club for a forearm—then you'd be crying about that, too!"*

The man moved closer, his chest puffed out, and Beau, almost 5 inches shorter, refused to back down. His eyes burned with fury as he barked, *"So fuck off! Don't come down here and disrespect my kid because yours got outworked."*

"Your wrestler was showboating!" the man spat, his voice rising.

"Showboating?" Beau roared, his fists clenching. *"Yeah, the one-arm man was showboating!"*

For a moment, it looked like they might actually come to blows. Beau stood his ground, shoulders squared, daring the man to make the next move. The tension hung thick in the air until a tournament official intervened, stepping between them and diffusing the situation.

Beau turned away, his voice still sharp as he called over his shoulder, "*Go back to the stands and stay there. You're out of your depth.*"

To his wrestlers, Beau was more than a coach. He was a warrior, always ready to go to battle for them, on the mat or off it. That day, they didn't just see his fiery devotion; they felt it.

As Tyler reached the other side of the mat, a few younger wrestlers paused mid-drill, casting quick glances his way before returning to their tasks. Tyler felt their judgment, silent but heavy. Tightening his grip on the worn strap of his duffel bag, he reminded himself that this was his chance. His first real opportunity to prove to Coach Beau and the team that he belonged. That he wasn't just some screw-up clinging to past glories.

Finding a quiet corner, Tyler dropped his bag and began his stretches, tuning out the murmurs around him. Beau hadn't arrived yet, but his presence already loomed, an invisible pressure that hung in the air.

"Alright, let's get started!" Beau's voice cut through the gym like a knife. He strode in with his trademark clipboard, his sharp eyes scanning the room. Conversations stopped instantly.

Beau's gaze landed on Tyler for a brief moment before moving on. "Warm-ups are over. On the line."

Tyler jogged to his place among the others. The whistle blew, and the team launched into sprints, bear crawls, and army crawls. Tyler's lungs burned, his legs screaming, but he refused to falter. Every step felt like a battle, every movement a declaration: *I belong here.*

"Faster, Bennett! Harder, Bagwell! Tyler, keep your damn hips down!" Beau barked.

Tyler adjusted, forcing his body lower despite the fire in his muscles. He caught Johnny Bennett smirking at him out of the corner of his eye and clenched his jaw. Approval didn't matter. Survival did.

The drills transitioned to technique work. Beau demonstrated a slick takedown setup, his movements sharp and deliberate. "This is wrestling," he said, gesturing to the circle. "Not whatever garbage you've been doing in the offseason. Show me you've still got it, or don't bother showing up tomorrow."

Tyler partnered with Alex; a lanky sophomore whose wide eyes betrayed his nerves. They cycled through the drills, Tyler focusing on every detail of Beau's instructions. But no matter how clean he tried to be, Beau's sharp eyes found every flaw.

"Tyler, you call that a sprawl?" Beau's voice exploded across the gym, laced with frustration. "Do it again! Slam your goddamn hips down like you're trying to break his spine. Whizzer in and press your palm into the back of his head—hard—drive his face into the mat until he's eating it. Don't hold back, dammit! You want to act soft, go join the chess club. Show you've got a pair and prove to me you belong on this team, because right now, you don't!"

Tyler gritted his teeth, repeating the motion. His body screamed for rest, but he pushed on. By the time Beau moved on, Tyler's shirt clung to him like a second skin, his breaths coming in ragged gasps.

Then came the gauntlet: "Bull in the Ring", a brutal takedown drill designed to push wrestlers past their breaking point. One man stood in the center, the bull, facing a relentless stream of fresh opponents until they could not go on. It was not something Beau used often, usually saved for punishment after a poor showing at a meet. But this was the first practice, and Tyler could not make sense of why Beau was pulling it out now.

"Tyler, you're our first bull of the season," Beau called, his tone unreadable.

Tyler's stomach dropped as he heard his name. He had not even considered that he might be the one called out. As he stepped forward, the weight of Beau's gaze bore down on him, and it became clear. This was not just a drill. It was a challenge.

Tyler stepped into the circle as the gym closed in around him. The first opponent lunged, and Tyler met him with a sharp sprawl, driving the kid's head hard into the mat. The second opponent came faster, testing Tyler's endurance. By the fourth, his legs felt like lead, sweat dripping into his eyes and blurring his vision.

"Keep fighting!" Beau shouted. "This is where you show me what you're made of."

The fifth opponent, Johnny Bennett, stepped in with a grin that promised pain. Johnny shot in low, and Tyler barely countered, twisting out of the takedown just in time. The effort left him gasping, but he stayed on his feet.

By the sixth opponent, Tyler's body screamed for him to stop. But he didn't. He couldn't. The gym became a blur of noise and movement, and when the final whistle blew, Tyler collapsed to his knees, chest heaving.

*****

Practice ended with conditioning drills, Beau's whistle cutting through the air like a metronome of misery. Tyler pushed through, his mind flashing back to Beau's words from last season: *"You don't wrestle alone. You better learn that, or it'll break you."*

As the team filed out, Tyler stayed behind, catching Beau's attention.

"What, Tyler?" Beau growled.

"I'd like to finish our talk."

"Then talk."

"I'm in."

"In what, Tyler? I'm trying to get out of here—I've got to meet Rosalyn and a wedding photographer. Just say it - you want 130, right?"

"Yeah."

"And your mom?"

"She said if you think I can do it, she believes it too."

"And Robby and Johnny?"

"Huh?" Tyler cocked his head like a confused dog, making Beau laugh. The coach pointed behind Tyler.

"Those two wingnuts—do they have your back?"

"Yeah, we even went to Shaw's last week to figure out how to make this suck a little less."

"Good luck with that. It's going to completely suck, but at least you've got them in your corner." Beau almost smiled. "Oh, and let me tell you what I told Robby in Shaw's that night: putting anything on top of a rice cake defeats the purpose of the rice cake. You'll need to learn to like your styrofoam *dry*."

Beau laughed as he walked away, amused at his own joke.

As he left the gym, the soreness in his body felt like a badge of honor. For the first time in months, Tyler believed he could do this. He could rebuild himself, piece by piece. And maybe, just maybe, he could reconnect with the team along the way.

Chapter Nine —
Frustration and Doubt - Now

I'm walking down the line
That divides me somewhere in my mind
Green Day - "Boulevard of Broken Dreams"

Bryce stood near the edge of the mat; his arms crossed tightly as the team cycled through drills. The gym buzzed with movement, but it felt like static electricity in his ears. His gaze lingered on his teammates, their forms sloppy, their energy lackluster. They weren't just losing matches; they were losing faith. And deep down, Bryce wasn't sure he could blame them.

Nick's face flashed in his mind again. The pale defeated look in his eyes after that day in the locker room still haunted Bryce. He'd done what he thought was right by going to Principal Owens, but the fallout had been brutal. His team gutted, their season cut short, and the weight of it all placed squarely on his shoulders. Leaders set the standard; he'd told himself at the time. But now? Now he wasn't so sure he even wanted to lead.

"Bryce, what was that?" Tyler's voice broke through his thoughts. He snapped his attention back to the present, realizing he'd just shoved Nick again during a drill. The younger wrestler stumbled, his face flushing with embarrassment.

"Nick's not trying hard enough," Bryce muttered, his tone flat.

Tyler's jaw tightened as he stepped forward. "Neither are you," he said sharply. "Your job isn't to humiliate your partner; it's to make him better."

Bryce scoffed, crossing his arms. "Maybe he's just not cut out for it."

The gym fell silent. All eyes turned toward the confrontation, the tension thick in the air. Tyler's expression hardened, but his voice remained steady. "Everyone starts somewhere, Bryce. Including you. Run it again."

Bryce hesitated, then begrudgingly returned to his stance. He went through the drill with stiff, robotic movements, his frustration palpable. Tyler watched closely, his grip tightening on the clipboard in his hand. Bryce's defiance was like a wall, and Tyler knew he had to find a way to break through.

After practice, Tyler called Bryce over as the rest of the team filed out. "What's going on with you?" he asked, his tone firm but calm.

Bryce leaned against the wall, avoiding his father's gaze. "What do you mean?"

"You know exactly what I mean," Tyler said. "You're shutting down. You're undermining everything I'm trying to do here."

Bryce's jaw tightened. "Maybe because I didn't ask you to come back. You think I want to be here, doing this? After everything that happened last season?"

Tyler exhaled; his frustration evident. "I get it. You're angry. But taking it out on the team isn't going to fix anything."

Bryce's eyes flashed with resentment. "You think this is about the team? It's about trust. They knew what was happening, and they did nothing. And now we're all supposed to trust you to make it better?"

Tyler paused, letting the words sink in. "You're right. What happened shouldn't have. And maybe I'm not the perfect person for this job, but I'm here because I believe this team can be better. I believe you can be better."

Bryce looked away, his fists clenching. Tyler stepped closer, lowering his voice. "You've got a choice, Bryce. You can keep fighting me, or you can help me rebuild this team. Either way, I'm not giving up on you."

For a long moment, Bryce didn't move. Finally, he shrugged, his voice barely audible. "We'll see."

As the gym emptied and the lights dimmed, Tyler watched Bryce walk away. It wasn't much, but it was a start.

Chapter Ten – The Loss

And you always seem outnumbered
You don't dare make a stand
Metallica– "Turn the Page"

The crowd's cheers were faint and scattered, barely masking the tension that hung over the gym. Tyler stood at the edge of the mat, watching as his team struggled match after match. The scoreboard painted a grim picture: Riverstone was being dismantled.

Bryce's match was one of the few bright spots. He stepped onto the mat with his usual confidence and dominated, his movements sharp and calculated. When the referee raised his hand, Tyler clapped politely, but the victory felt hollow. Bryce didn't acknowledge his teammates as he walked off, his focus solely on his water bottle and the bench.

When the meet ended, the final tally was brutal. Tyler gathered the team near the bleachers, his expression somber but resolute. "This wasn't about losing," he began, his voice carrying over the murmurs. "It was about how we lost. About giving up on ourselves and each other. That's what hurts the most."

The team shifted uncomfortably, avoiding his gaze. Bryce leaned against the wall, arms crossed, his face unreadable.

On the bus ride home, the silence was heavy. Tyler sat near the front, replaying the meet in his mind. Behind him way in the back, Bryce sat with his earbuds in, staring out the window. The distance between them felt like miles.

When the bus pulled into the school parking lot, Tyler waited as the wrestlers filed off. Bryce lingered at the back; his movements deliberate.

"Bryce, stay back," Tyler said, his tone leaving no room for argument.

Bryce paused, then turned slowly. "What?"

Tyler stepped in closer, his voice low but firm. "Tonight wasn't about the loss. It was about how you handled it. Or didn't."

Bryce's jaw tightened. "I wrestled my match. I won. That's all anyone expects."

"No," Tyler said, shaking his head. "That's not all. The team's looking to you, Bryce. Whether you like it or not, they're following your lead. And right now, you're leading them nowhere."

Bryce's eyes narrowed. "Maybe I don't want them following me. Maybe I don't want any of this."

Tyler's expression softened, but his voice remained steady. "Then stop pretending. If you're going to be here, be here. Otherwise, step aside and let someone else lead."

Bryce didn't respond. He shoved his earbuds back in and stepped down out of the bus doors, his posture rigid. Tyler watched him go, a mix of frustration and determination churning in his chest.

Later that night, Tyler sat alone in the empty gym, the silence pressing in around him. He stared at the mat where so many battles had been fought, both physical and emotional. Bryce's words echoed in his mind, and he couldn't shake the feeling that this wasn't just about wrestling. It was about trust, about rebuilding something broken.

"We'll get there," Tyler murmured to himself, the faintest glimmer of hope lighting the darkness.

Chapter Eleven - Tyler: Junior Year - The Quest

Who you tryna get crazy with, ese?
Don't you know I'm loco?
Cypress Hill – "Insane in the Brain"

The bus ride back to Riverstone was dead silent, every wrestler staring at the floor or out the window, avoiding Coach Beau's piercing gaze. Tyler sat in the middle row, his legs bouncing with nervous energy. His match had been a disaster, a loss that stung even more because of how he'd handled it afterward. The image of the water bottle flying from his hand and the hollow thud as it hit the wall played on a loop in his mind.

When the bus pulled into the school parking lot, Beau stood silently, letting the wrestlers file off first. He manned the door like a gatekeeper, his sharp eyes scanning each one as they passed. Tyler tried to slip past without making eye contact, but Beau's voice stopped him cold.

"Don't get too comfortable," Beau said, his tone clipped. "We've got some things to sort out tomorrow."

Tyler swallowed hard and nodded, following the others into the cold night. Once the team was gathered outside, Beau didn't waste time.

"I'm not here to be your friend, and I don't give a shit if you like me," Beau said, his voice cutting through the crisp air. "But you will not waste my time with such a half-assed effort as what you showed tonight."

57

His gaze landed squarely on Tyler. "Tyler, you got your ass handed to you, but you still had enough energy to throw a tantrum and chuck your water bottle. Let me ask you something. Why the hell didn't you use that energy on the mat to finish a single fucking shot?"

Tyler's stomach churned, but Beau didn't wait for an answer.

"Tomorrow, don't bother bringing your headgear. No drilling, no live wrestling. Just The Quest." Beau's tone left no room for argument. The team felt the weight of his words— the determination in him this season was ratcheting up, and they could sense it. Whatever Beau was carrying, it was heavy.

*****

The next day, the gym felt colder and quieter than usual. The team gathered on the mats, their faces pale with apprehension. Beau stood at the edge, holding the infamous deck of index cards in his hands, his expression unreadable. Tyler recognized those cards immediately; their frayed edges spoke of hours of punishment. He'd seen them only once before, as a freshman, but this time, something felt different.

Beau knelt on the mat in full view of the team and began pulling *"rest"* cards from the deck, tearing each one cleanly in half. The sound of ripping paper echoed through the gym, almost obscene in the silence. In their place, he slid in more of the brutal cards: sets of one hundred hit-its, fifty push-ups, and other grueling exercises. When he finished, Beau stacked the cards deliberately and set them down just inside the boundary line of the mat.

"There's no mercy in this deck," Beau said, his voice low but cutting. "This match will last the whole practice. By the end of it, we'll see who actually wants to be here."

Tyler's heart sank as Beau circled the team like a predator. Stories of The Quest from Beau's days of wrestling at Salem High were infamous, and now those stories were coming to life. The deck wasn't just a collection of exercises, it was a weapon. Each card turned physical exhaustion into mental torment, leaving the wrestlers to imagine what fresh hell might come next.

Beau shuffled the deck, letting the tension build before he spoke again. His eyes landing on Tyler. "Nobody disrespects this team, this program, or me. Today, you're going to learn what it means to earn your place on this mat."

He flipped the first card. "Thirty push-ups."

The wrestlers dropped immediately, their grunts filling the air as they counted. Tyler's arms burned by the time he hit twenty, but he refused to falter. Around him, the sounds of labored breathing echoed through the gym.

"Fifty jumping jacks," Beau called, his voice slicing through their gasps for air.

The wrestlers moved in unison, though their movements became more ragged with every jump. Tyler glanced at the younger wrestlers, noting the panic in their eyes as the realization of how long this was going to last began to sink in.

Beau knelt again, flipping the next card. "Rest," he announced, his tone mocking. Holding the card up for effect, he slowly tore it in half and let the pieces drift to the ground.

"You think you've earned rest?" Beau asked, his eyes narrowing. "Screw that. Fifty hit-its."

An hour in, the mat was slick with sweat. Tyler's shirt clung to his back, and his legs wobbled as he dropped into another set of hit-its. Around him, wrestlers collapsed between reps, their bodies trembling with fatigue. Beau didn't yell; he didn't have to. His sharp, unrelenting presence alone drove them forward.

By the second hour, the deck had become a symbol of dread. Each card revealed another punishment, and the exercises stacked up with no end in sight. Tyler's body screamed at him to stop, but he refused to quit. He stole glances at his teammates whenever his resolve faltered. The veterans gritted their teeth and pushed through, while the younger wrestlers teetered on the edge of collapse. No one dared to break. No one dared to cry.

When the final card was flipped and the last set of exercises completed, the wrestlers collapsed onto the mat, their bodies spent. Tyler lay flat on his back, staring at the ceiling, his chest heaving. His arms felt like lead, his legs numb, but he was still there. They all were.

Beau loomed over them, his hands planted on his hips. "I'm not here to win a popularity contest," he said, his tone even but resolute. "Liking me isn't part of the deal. Winning is. One day, obviously not today, you'll understand why this matters."

The wrestlers staggered to their feet, some leaning on each other for support as they filed out of the gym. Tyler hung back, watching the group shuffle toward the locker room. Despite the exhaustion, something felt different. The shared suffering had left its mark, binding them in ways words never could.

For the first time, Tyler began to understand what Beau had been trying to do. He wasn't there to break them. He was there to show them that by leaning on each other, they could become unbreakable as a team.

Chapter Twelve - Coach's Way

Well, it's midnight, damn right,
we're wound up too tight
Nickleback – "Burn it to the Ground"

Bryce didn't know what to expect from his dad as the team filed in for practice. They hadn't spoken since Bryce had left the gym the night before. He had purposely stayed out late, heading to Manchester after the meet to discuss the season with Johnson.

"This team is lost," Johnson said pointedly as they ordered an after-match snack at the Red Arrow Diner.

"I don't know that it's fixable. Or if it's even worth it. I see nothing in the eyes of the team that says they care. I'm not sure why we're bothering with a season," Bryce said, defeated.

"That's not what I meant. I meant this team is lost, and you need to fix it," Johnson snapped. "You said you were going to take the heat, that you would wear this. Well, this isn't how I want our senior year to go. We sacrificed last year for this team; why are you sacrificing this year too?"

"Sacrificing this year on us? What the hell is that supposed to mean? I didn't choose what we saw last year, and I'm not responsible for rebuilding it."

"If not you, Bryce, then who?" Johnson knew that question would sting Bryce's pride. "You were right to go to Owens last year; I should have stood beside you. But now,

those underclassmen you think don't want to hear from you are watching everything you do. If this team is to have a chance, you need to be the one that shows them how to buy into what your dad is preaching. He's speaking a language of hope and opportunity, but if you're not listening, no one else will."

Johnson's words hung over Bryce as their Boston cream pies arrived. The sight of the legendary oversized slices broke the tension as they looked at the plates in front of them.

"Well... given how tonight went, I'm pretty sure my dad's going to run us into the ground like Beau used to do to his team anytime the effort didn't meet his standards," Bryce said, glancing at Johnson. "I think we'll have no problem working off these calories. And I hear what you're saying. Tomorrow, we start showing them the right way to work."

*****

A heavy silence weighed over the team as they quietly stretched on the mat, awaiting their coach and the inevitable consequence of their lackluster effort the night before. No one looked sharp; even Bryce, despite his win, had been sloppy and seemed to be just going through the motions. Johnson at least, was showing commitment and energy, but no one looked to him for direction, they focused on Bryce.

Johnson had made it clear to Bryce last night that he needed to step up or this season was already done.

Bryce noticed Tyler leaning against the wall, arms crossed, watching the team, his face showing a mixture of frustration and hope. The loss had cut deep, but what lingered was the way they had fallen apart, not just as individuals but as a team. Tyler had decided today wasn't about punishment; it was about finding a way forward.

Taking a deep breath, Tyler walked to the center of the mat.

"Listen up," he called, his voice calm but firm.

The team shuffled into a circle around him, their faces guarded. Tyler waited for the silence to settle before speaking.

"Yesterday wasn't about losing," he began. "Losing happens. It's part of our sport. What matters is how you respond to it. And yesterday?" He paused, scanning their faces. "We didn't respond very well. We gave up—not just on ourselves, but on each other."

A few wrestlers looked away, their expressions tightening. Bryce kept his gaze fixed on the mat in front of him.

"I'm not my old coach, Coach Beau," Tyler continued, his voice steady. "I'm not here to break you down and make you hate me enough to fight for each other, because that's how he responded when we gave an effort like you did last night. But I'm not here to break you; I'm here to make you better. And that means we need to commit, not just to the sport, but to each other."

Tyler reached into his pocket and pulled out a pen. "I want each of you to think about one thing you can do to make this team stronger. One thing. And I want you to write it down." He gestured to a stack of small cards he'd placed on the mat beside him. "We'll keep these, and we'll hold each other accountable to them."

There was a moment of hesitation before Bryce stepped forward, picking up a card and pen. Slowly, the others followed. Tyler watched as they wrote, their expressions shifting from reluctance to quiet determination.

The practice that followed was different. Tyler had paired the wrestlers strategically, veterans with younger teammates, partners who didn't usually work together. The drills weren't just about technique; they were about communication and support. Tyler moved between the pairs, offering encouragement and corrections where needed.

"Good sprawl, Nick," Tyler said as the lean sophomore executed the move. "Bryce, help him tighten that whizzer. Show him how to use it to rotate his opponent's shoulder deeper into the mat as he circles."

This time, Bryce didn't hesitate. His body language was upbeat, something neither Tyler nor the rest of the team expected. He crouched down beside Nick. "You need to get lower," Bryce said, his tone constructive. "Brace with your free forearm like this, resting your weight down on the guy's head."

Nick mimicked the motion, struggling to balance as he shifted his position. Bryce laughed playfully, not dismissively, and adjusted Nick's arm himself. "No, not like that. Here. Now pinch his shoulder between your biceps and your chest. Put pressure down with your shoulder into his, like you're trying to pop it out of the socket."

Nick nodded, trying again. Bryce was watching, his brow furrowed in concentration. Tyler noticed the moment Bryce softened, just slightly, as Nick finally executed the move correctly.

"Better," Bryce said, stepping back. "Don't forget to pivot hard."

There was genuine enthusiasm from Bryce. He moved back into position, and Tyler caught the faint flicker of approval on Nick's face.

By the end of practice, the atmosphere had shifted. The wrestlers weren't just teammates anymore; they were starting to act in unison. Tyler gathered them in a circle again, this time standing among them.

"Today was better," he said simply. "But better isn't good enough. We've got work to do—together. Keep showing up for each other, and we'll get there."

As the team broke for conditioning, something surprising happened. The veterans started cheering on the younger wrestlers, clapping and shouting encouragement. When one wrestler lagged behind during sprints, another dropped back to run beside him, urging him not to quit. Tyler stood at the edge of the mat, arms crossed, taking it all in.

For the first time, the team was moving as one. And for the first time, Tyler felt like they might just have a shot.

After practice, Tyler lingered in the gym, appreciating the new level of commitment seen from the team today. Most of the team had cleared out, but he noticed Nick hovering near the door, his bag slung over one shoulder.

"Something on your mind, Nick?" Tyler asked, looking up.

Nick hesitated, then walked over. "I just wanted to say... thanks. For today. I think— I mean, I think I'm getting better."

"You are," Tyler said, smiling. "Keep working with Bryce. He's tough, but he knows what he's doing."

Nick nodded, his expression thoughtful. "He's not as bad as he tries to be."

Tyler chuckled. "Don't tell him that. He'll deny it." But as Nick walked away, Tyler found himself thinking about what Nick had said. It reminded him of something Coach Beau had drilled into them long ago: true character isn't always obvious at first glance. Beau used to say that under pressure, when the stakes were high, people showed you who they really were. Tyler could hear his voice even now, calm and resolute. *"Give people time, and they'll show you what they're made of."*

As Nick left, Bryce walked by, his earbuds dangling around his neck. Tyler called out, stopping him.

"Bryce."

Bryce paused; head turned slightly over his shoulder. "What?"

"Good work today," Tyler said simply.

Bryce nodded slowly and gave an odd little grin. "Yeah. Thanks."

It was brief, almost insignificant, but to Tyler, it was everything. He watched Bryce leave, the gym quiet once again. The road ahead was long, but today, he'd seen something he hadn't seen in weeks: commitment.

Chapter Thirteen - Father and Son

Boy, don't worry, you'll find yourself
Follow your heart and nothing else
Shinedown – "Simple Man"

The house was quiet when Tyler pulled into the driveway, the soft crunch of gravel under his tires the only sound in the cold night air. Bryce's car was already parked, a thin layer of frost forming on the windshield. Tyler sat for a moment, staring at the dimly lit windows. He liked what had started to spark at practice today, but was it truly a sign of hope or just a fleeting moment of Bryce's love for the sport overshadowing his frustration with last season?

He stepped into the house, setting his bag down by the door. The faint sound of a video game came from Bryce's room, punctuated by rapid button clicks and muffled frustration. Tyler sighed, pulling off his jacket and hanging it on the hook. He debated whether to let Bryce cool off or face the tension head-on.

After a moment, he walked down the hall and knocked lightly on Bryce's door. The clicking stopped.

"Yeah?" Bryce's voice came, muffled but audible.

Tyler pushed the door open slightly and poked his head inside. Bryce was sprawled on his bed, a controller in hand, the glow of the TV screen reflecting on his face. He didn't look up.

"Got a minute?" Tyler asked, leaning against the doorframe.

Bryce shrugged. "Sure. What's up?"

Tyler stepped inside, pulling over the desk chair and sitting down. He let a beat of silence pass before speaking. "How do you think practice went today?"

Bryce paused his game, finally looking up. "I think it was a good start, but we have a way to go to be the team we can be."

"Really?" Tyler raised an eyebrow.

Bryce set the controller down and leaned back against the headboard. "Dad, Johnson and I had a straightforward convo last night. He called me out, and he was right. Last year is done. You aren't them; this team isn't the problem. Basically, Johnson told me it was time to pull my head out of my ass and start being the leader I told him I was last year."

Tyler laughed, the sound breaking the tension in the room. "So, Johnson's doing my job for me now?"

Bryce smirked, his expression lightening. "Apparently. Guess I needed to hear it from someone who doesn't share my last name."

"Well, I'll take it," Tyler said, shaking his head. "I'm impressed, Bryce. It takes a lot to own up to that, even more to act on it."

Bryce shifted, his smirk fading. "I'm sorry, Dad. I've had a hard time this year, and I shouldn't keep shutting you out." His voice grew heavier. "I've been having a tough time with all of this. I hate looking at the sophomores. And the juniors—I have no idea who else went through what Nick did."

Tyler leaned forward, his elbows resting on his knees. "Bryce, you did the right thing. You have nothing to feel bad about."

"I should've done more."

Tyler sighed. "I get it. I felt the same way about my cousin, Jacob. I thought I should've done more to protect him. But it wasn't my job Bryce, and protecting the freshmen wasn't yours. What matters now is what you do moving forward—for this team, for yourself, for Johnson, and the other seniors. Be their leader. Show them how to do the right thing, like you did for Nick. Not just the wrestler who kicks ass on the mat, but the guy who walked into Principal Owen's office and sacrificed his own shot at a state title to protect others."

Bryce looked away, his voice quieter. "I'm trying, Dad. I'm going to try to be better connected to the team, but right now... I don't feel very connected at all."

Chapter Fourteen - Tyler: Junior Year — A Hint of Respect

So take the photographs and still frames in your mind
Hang it on a shelf in good health and good time
Green Day – "Good Riddance"

Parents, students, and rival teams packed the bleachers, their voices blending into a chaotic roar. Tyler stood off to the side of the mat, headgear dangling from one hand as he stretched his shoulders. Cutting to 130 lbs had been grueling, but now that he was here, he needed to prove it was worth it, not just to Coach Beau but to himself.

As the 125-match started, Tyler stared across the mat. His opponent, a seasoned senior with a reputation for grinding opponents down, was warming up with sharp, deliberate movements. Tyler's stomach churned, but he forced himself to focus, narrowing his eyes as he visualized the first takedown.

"On your toes… stay aggressive… control the pace," Robby's voice cut through the noise, trying to get Tyler locked in. Robby had just finished six brutal minutes of his own, winning with a last-second head throw.

"Robby, go get a drink and towel off, man… you stink," Johnny teased, grinning. He turned to Tyler. "Ty, just wrestle your match. You've done the work—now's the fun part."

That was a Coach Beau line. Meets were the reward: a chance to show off your moves in front of friends, maybe smile at the girls in the stands as you pinned your opponent. Practice was the grind. Wrestling under the light was the payoff.

"Tyler!" Coach Beau's voice sliced through the noise. Tyler jogged over, heart pounding. Beau didn't say much, he didn't need to. He locked eyes with Tyler and muttered, "You know what to do. Get it done."

Tyler nodded, swallowing hard, and stepped onto the mat. The referee signaled for the wrestlers to shake hands. Tyler's palm met his opponent's, firm and unyielding. The whistle blew, and the match began.

The first period was a blur of motion and strain. Tyler found himself on the defensive almost immediately, sprawling just in time to block a takedown. His counterattack lacked conviction, and they reset, circling each other like predators. The crowd's cheers faded into a dull roar in Tyler's ears.

"You need actual effort, Tyler! Commit to your counters!" Beau barked, flailing his arms on the edge of the mat. "If you didn't want to wrestle, why'd you bother cutting the weight?"

Tommy Bennett, the best of the Bennett brothers at impersonating Beau, loved reenacting Beau's signature move: turning his back and throwing his arms up when someone missed an opportunity. Beau's methods seemed harsh, but they grounded his wrestlers.

He wasn't like Mr. Kane, Snake, who had mentored Beau as a boy. Snake had once found an eight-year-old Beau crying after being teased, offering words that changed his trajectory. Snake had been Beau's light, but Beau's fire burned hotter. Still, his connection to his wrestlers was real. If you gave everything on the mat, win or lose, Beau lifted you up. If you made excuses, he would let you hear it.

"If you don't want the ref to decide the match, pin your opponent," he'd say. *"Don't give them a chance to do anything but slap the mat and raise your arm."*

By the end of the first period, the score was tied at zero, but Tyler felt like he had wrestled an entire match. He circled back toward the corner, gasping for air. Beau stood there, arms crossed, expression unreadable.

"You're out there waiting," Beau said bluntly. "News flash, Sparky: he's not handing you anything. You want this? Go get it."

Tyler wiped the sweat from his face, the sting of Beau's words pushing him harder. Tyler started the second period on bottom. This time, he exploded off the whistle, breaking free for the first point of the match. The crowd roared. Confidence surged through him as he reset. When his opponent came harder, Tyler matched his intensity, landing a clean single-leg takedown to go up 3-0.

But in the final seconds of the period, his opponent's relentless pace wore him down. An escape followed by a quick takedown caused the lead to evaporate.

At the start of the third period, with the match tied 3-3, Tyler's opponent selected neutral. As he put his right foot on the green line Tyler heard Johnny call from behind the bench, "Find your opening, Tyler!"

Tyler locked eyes with his opponent. Both were drenched in sweat, their movements slower now, but no less determined. The whistle blew and the gladiators resumed their hand fighting. Circling, stepping in, moving back, each of them shifting quickly trying to catch the other out of position. Neither wrestler able to gain an inch.

With time running out, Tyler saw it. His opponent's stance shifted too high, his weight leaning forward. Tyler shot in, wrapping the leg with precision. He drove through, muscles screaming, forcing his opponent to the mat. The whistle blew. Takedown. The gym erupted, but Tyler barely heard it. He had done it.

The final score: 5-3!

Tyler collapsed onto the mat, chest heaving as he stared at the ceiling. His opponent stood, face flushed and extended a hand. Tyler took it, allowing himself to be pulled to his feet. The referee raised his arm, and the crowd roared again, the sound washing over him like a wave.

Walking back to his corner, Tyler's legs trembled with exhaustion. Coach Beau was waiting. For a moment, Tyler thought Beau might offer rare praise. Instead, Beau gave a small nod.

"You earned it," Beau said, gruff but approving. Tyler nodded back, pride flickering inside him. At the edge of the mat, his teammates cheered and celebrated. For the first time in a long time, he felt like he belonged.

In the locker room afterward, the energy buzzed. Teammates slapped his back, replaying the match's key moments between shared jokes. Tyler smiled, but as he sat unlacing his shoes, a quiet thought crept in.

Winning today was one thing. Staying here, maintaining this level, was another.

As he slung his bag over his shoulder and headed toward the gym doors, he caught Coach Beau's eye once more. Beau didn't speak, but the look was clear: *This is just the beginning.*

Tyler nodded to himself. He was ready for it. At least, he thought he was.

Chapter Fifteen – The Injury

Sometimes, I feel the fear of uncertainty stinging clear
Incubus – "Drive"

The Riverstone team gathered for their pre-match huddle. Tyler stood in the center. He scanned the determined faces around him. This was one of their biggest dual meets of the season, a chance to prove they could compete with the best.

"Tonight's about trust," Tyler said, his voice steady and calm. "Trust in yourselves, trust in each other, and trust in the work we've put in. Win or lose, we leave everything on the mat."

The wrestlers nodded, their focus sharpening. Bryce stood stoic. His arms crossed, listening quietly. At the far side of the huddle, Johnson, the team's 165-pounder, was bouncing on the balls of his feet, his energy almost too high. Johnson was one of their most consistent wrestlers all season, and tonight he was up against the top-ranked 165lbs wrestler in the state.

"I'm ready," Johnson said, his voice carrying a nervous edge. "This guy's tough, but I've got him."

Tyler gave him a reassuring nod. "Stay focused, wrestle your match, and you'll be fine."

The meet began with the lightweights, and Riverstone came out strong, taking an early lead. Bryce delivered a dominant performance, pinning his opponent in the second period and setting the tone for the middleweights. The team was riding high as Johnson stepped onto the mat for his match.

The first period was a tense back-and-forth dance, with neither wrestler gaining a clear advantage. Johnson's quickness kept him in the match, but his opponent's strength was evident in every tie-up.

The second period started with Johnson in the down position. He exploded off the whistle, fighting for hand control as he worked to escape. The crowd roared as he spun out and earned a point, but his opponent countered immediately, driving Johnson toward the edge of the mat.

Then it happened. In the middle of a scramble, Johnson planted his left leg awkwardly to resist a takedown. His knee bent in a direction it shouldn't have, and a sharp, audible pop echoed through the gym. Johnson cried out in pain as he collapsed to the mat, clutching his knee as the referee blew the whistle to stop the match.

Tyler was on the mat in an instant, his heart racing. The trainer hurried over, kneeling beside Johnson as the gym fell into an uneasy silence. Johnson's face was pale, his hands gripping his knee as tears streamed down his face. "It's my knee," he choked out, wincing with every word. "I can't move it."

The trainer gently examined the knee, her expression grim. "It's bad," she said quietly to Tyler. "It's likely an ACL tear, based on how it bent. I cannot see how he's not done for the season."

Tyler felt a wave of emotions crash over him, concern for Johnson, frustration at the sudden blow to the team, and a gnawing fear about what this meant for their season. He leaned closer to Johnson, keeping his voice calm. "We're going to get you taken care of. You did great out there, Johnson. Let's focus on getting you healthy."

The trainer signaled for help, and together they lifted Johnson off the mat and onto a stretcher. The crowd applauded softly as he was carried out, but the energy in the gym had shifted. The team sat in stunned silence; their earlier momentum completely gone.

The remaining matches were a blur of missed opportunities and half-hearted efforts. Riverstone lost the dual meet decisively, and by the time the team filed into the locker room, the mood was as heavy as the air after a storm.

Tyler stood at the edge of the room, watching as the wrestlers sat slumped on the benches, their heads down. Bryce leaned against his locker, his face a mix of frustration and something harder to read.

"Listen up," Tyler said, his voice cutting through the silence. The team looked up reluctantly, their eyes weary. "What happened tonight was tough. Losing Johnson is a blow, and it's okay to feel that. But this season isn't over. Not by a long shot."

He let his gaze settle on Bryce. "We need to step up. All of us. Bryce, that means you too. This team is looking to you. It's time to decide what kind of leader you want to be."

Bryce didn't respond, his jaw tightening as he looked away. Tyler dismissed the team, the room sinking into heavy silence.

He noticed Bryce lingering at his locker while the others filed out, their footsteps echoing in the empty gym. Tyler approached, keeping his tone steady.

"I know this isn't what you signed up for," he said quietly. "But this is where it counts. The team needs you, Bryce. If you bump up to 165, Nick can fill your spot, earn us some points, and we can still fight for the championship— together. Stay at 150, and you'll probably win states. But it'll just be you."

Bryce finally met his eyes, his expression a mix of frustration and doubt. "I'll think about it."

Tyler nodded. It wasn't the answer he wanted, but it was a start. As Bryce walked out, Tyler remained, staring at the empty locker room. The air felt still and heavy. The road ahead had just gotten tougher, but he wasn't ready to give up. Not yet.

Chapter Sixteen - Tyler: Junior Year - Monday before States

If I could relive those days
I know the one thing that would never change
Nickleback - "Photograph"

The Monday before the State tourney started with a brutal workout. Coach Beau's whistle echoed sharply through the gym, driving the team through drill after drill. "Faster! Move! Quick! No stopping!" he barked, his voice cutting through their labored breaths. Tyler glanced at his teammates; their eyes were heavy with exhaustion, silently pleading for mercy. But Coach Beau never wavered.

Finally, after what felt like an eternity, he blew the whistle one last time. "Roll 'em up! Meeting in the team room in five minutes!"

The team dragged themselves into the room, sweat-soaked and drained. On the whiteboard at the front of the room, a new list caught everyone's attention: each weight class, their names, and the minimum finishes needed for the team to win its first state championship.

Coach Beau stood in front of the board; his voice unusually measured. "Gentlemen, we have a few things to go over before we call it a night," he began. "First, this is our roadmap to a championship. Coach Mitchell and I decided to lay it out clearly. Under each weight, you'll see what we need from you. This is how we win our first team title."

Tyler's eyes scanned the list until they landed on his weight class: "Semis, finish top 3." His stomach dropped. Ranked as the sixth seed in the 130-pound bracket, his first match would be against the third seed, a wrestler who had beaten him twice this season. If he lost, the team's dream of a championship might be over before it started.

Coach Beau continued, his tone growing firmer. "Everything on this board is achievable. Four days. That's how long we've got to make this happen. We've got banners hanging in this gym for the Bennett brothers, but this year? This year isn't about two or three people. This year, the team earns its banner. No offense, Bennetts, but it's time to share the spotlight."

. "Let's make it happen. I want to be part of at least one championship team before I graduate." Eddie called out from the back.

The room fell silent for a moment, Eddie's words carrying a weight everyone felt. Tyler glanced over at him, understanding how much the season had already cost Eddie but unaware of how much more it would take in the future. Eddie had pushed his way back onto the mat too soon after breaking his wrist in a heartbreaking football championship loss just a few months earlier, barely able to compete this season. Tyler, and everyone, knew the physical toll would stay with him long after high school, but no one expected what would happen. Two months after graduating from Riverstone, on the first day of orientation at the Naval Academy, Eddie's dream, he would be dismissed when it was discovered that he could not hold his grip on the rope during climbing drills.

Coach Beau nodded; his voice softer now. "I agree, Eddie. I think Bagwell would, too." He paused, taking in the room. "And I'll say this, I'd like nothing more than to see us raise that banner as my last act as your coach."

The words hit the team like a thunderclap.

"Unfortunately, this will be my last season here at Riverstone," he continued. "Balancing work and coaching has become impossible. I've tried, but I can't be at practice by 3:15 every day anymore. Coach Mitchell and I agreed you deserve to know before the tournament. No surprises."

The room was silent. No one really knew what they should say, Coach Beau hadn't ever hinted that he would ever leave. It sort of was assumed that he was early into a 40-year run at Riverstone.

"Well, that fucking sucks!" Robby muttered from the side, breaking the tension. Laughter rippled through the room, cutting the weight of the moment.

Coach Beau smirked. "I thought you might be happy, Robby. But I'm leaving The Quest behind with Coach Mitchell, so you'll still think of me next year."

Tyler, Johnny, and Robby exchanged quick glances, stifling grins. Unbeknownst to Coach Beau, during the last Quest, Johnny and Robby had swiped a few of the worst cards that defined the exercise. They'd hidden them for years behind a photo in Johnny's parents' basement, a small act of rebellion that Coach Beau wouldn't discover for decades. Years later, Coach Beau would receive a letter from Johnny, congratulating him on his new coaching job at St. Peter's. Inside the envelope, he'd find the missing cards, along with an apology and an explanation. *"We didn't hate The Quest as much as we let on,"* Johnny wrote. *"But we thought you'd like to know you were always on our minds."*

For now, though, the team sat silently in the room, each of them staring at the whiteboard and the weight of what lay ahead. Tyler glanced at his name again, the words "Semis, finish top 3" blurring in his mind. Four days. Four days to be the wrestler the team needed him to be.

"Gentlemen," Coach Beau said, his voice cutting through the silence, "my first season here, Bagwell and Eddie remember, we only had four varsity wrestlers go to State. The next month, the school board axed us to a club team, but your parents fundraised for this team. We started my second season here with six wrestlers, so I laid out a challenge, 'bring a friend to practice or we will just do conditioning for a month', and some of you, hell Johnny, you brought three friends just in case one of your teammates couldn't find anyone. Any of those friends who accepted the challenge to show up, became Riverstone wrestlers. You gentlemen have gone through punishing workouts, irrational expectations from a sometimes not-so-level-headed coach. But overall, overall, you grew into fine young men. Let's go win this…for each other. For this team. For that banner."

Chapter Seventeen – Self or Team?

Through all the years, through all the times
You stood by me
Creed – "My Sacrifice"

Bryce walked into the kitchen, the quiet of the house settling around him. He pulled out a chair and sat at the table, but after a moment, he got back up, crossing to the sink to fill a glass with water. The cold rush against his palm did little to steady the thoughts spinning in his head. *Do I stay at 150 for myself, or move up for the team?*

Winning states had been his goal all year. He could see it—his hand raised, the title his. But Johnson's absence had changed everything. Without someone at 165, the team didn't stand a chance.

But it's not your job to save everyone, a small voice whispered. Bryce ignored it.

As he sat back down, footsteps sounded behind him. Tyler walked in, rubbing his face like he hadn't slept much either.

"Can't sleep?" Tyler asked.

Bryce took a sip of water, then shrugged. "Just thinking."

"About states?"

Bryce hesitated, then nodded. "Yeah. And Johnson. And... the team."

Tyler sat down across from him. "It's a lot to carry."

Bryce said nothing.

"When I was a junior," Tyler continued, his voice low, "we were chasing a state title too. But we didn't have the firepower to pull it off. Beau asked me to suck down three weight classes to give us a shot. It was brutal. Beyond unhealthy. But I did it."

Bryce frowned. "Why would you do that to yourself?"

Tyler's eyes stayed fixed on the table, as if the answer was carved into the wood. "Because I thought I had to. I'd screwed up so much the year before. I turned my back on the team my sophomore year. Cutting weight was my way of making it up to them."

Bryce leaned back; arms crossed. "So, you sacrificed yourself to prove something?"

Tyler shook his head slowly. "That's what I told myself then. But it wasn't about proving anything. It was about what the team did for me."

Bryce blinked. "What do you mean?"

"They didn't give up on me, even when I gave them every reason to. Beau, the Bennetts, Robby, the freshmen— they stepped up when I didn't deserve it. They carried me, Bryce. And I wanted to carry them back."

Bryce looked down at his glass, tracing the rim with his finger. "You're saying I should do the same."

"I'm not saying anything," Tyler said, his voice steady. "I'm just telling you what happened. What you decide is up to you." He stood, resting a hand on Bryce's shoulder. "But leading isn't about feeling like you've done enough. It's about showing up when it counts."

Tyler left, his footsteps fading into the hall. Bryce sat alone, the weight of his father's words pressing on him like a stone.

*****

The next day, the gym buzzed with the chaotic energy of a late season practice. Bryce stood at the edge of the room, watching his teammates warm up. His stomach churned as he stepped forward.

"I've got something to say," he called out, his voice louder than he expected.

The room went silent, all eyes turning to him. Bryce swallowed hard.

"I'm moving up to 165 for states," he said firmly. "Johnson's spot needs filling, and I'll take it. Nick's wrestling 150. He's ready."

Nick, the athletic underclassman who had shadowed Bryce all season, gaped. "Me?! At 150?"

Bryce nodded. "You've earned it. The team needs this to win."

Murmurs rippled through the team before Tyler's voice cut through. "You heard him. Let's get to work."

As the wrestlers broke into drills, Tyler caught Bryce's eye. His son met his gaze and gave a small nod, jaw set with determination.

Tyler nodded back, pride swelling in his chest. Bryce wasn't just stepping up for the team, he was stepping into his own as a leader.

And for Tyler, that was the kind of victory worth fighting for.

Chapter Eighteen – Tyler: Junior Year – States – Quarterfinals

So don't mistake my kindness for weakness
'Cause I can flip that switch
And you can find out quick
Tyler Braden – "Devil You Know"

"Gentlemen," Coach Beau began, standing before his grapplers as they sat on the bleachers beneath the Riverstone Wrestling banner, sitting high above the mats spread out across the gym floor of Hollis-Brookline High School. The red-and-black flag bore the roaring Saber logo, an ever-present symbol of their pride and grit. "There is no doubt we'll be riding home with some hardware tonight." His words were confident, referring to medals and, hopefully, a team championship plaque.

"But before you take the mat, I want you to understand something," Beau continued. "It's something I learned during my last tournament under Mr. Kane." The wrestlers exchanged glances; they all noticed that whenever Beau spoke of his Boys Club coach, he never used the nickname "Snake," only "Mr. Kane."

"When I wrestled in the finals, a pin by me guaranteed we'd win the team championship. Anything else, and we might not. After my match, I broke down crying. Not because I lost; I hadn't. But because I felt like I'd failed Mr.

Kane, because I hadn't pinned my opponent. I thought I hadn't done enough to give him the championship he deserved."

The boys leaned in, surprised by their coach's candor. Beau rarely spoke about his own wrestling days, focusing instead on the techniques, positioning, and mindset they needed to succeed. And he never talked about crying.

"Mr. Kane asked me why I was crying. I told him I'd let him down, that I hadn't done enough. And do you know what he said to me?" Beau paused, his gaze moving over the wrestlers gathered before him. "He told me the day I walked into his room, ready to commit and asking to be one of his boys, I had already given him everything he ever wanted from me. All he wanted was for me to see there was a path forward. He said that the darkness I was stuck in, crying over some bullies, it had just been a temporary moment. He wanted me to see there are people who would provide a light forward. He said my wins were for me but helping me through the journey—that was his reward."

The wrestlers sat in silence, processing the story.

"What I'm saying to you is this: regardless of what happens with the team score, cherish your moments out there. You've earned the pride that comes with reaching whatever goals you've set for yourself. Focus on being the best version of yourself on the mat, and everything else will fall into place. Don't think for a second that you need to win this for me. The moment you accepted the challenge to be part of this generation of Riverstone Wrestling, you gave me the greatest gift I could ask for. So, thank you."

He smiled faintly; his eyes gleaming. "Now, in the immortal words of Al Bundy... 'Let's Rock.'"

The boys laughed, the tension breaking just enough.

*****

Tyler knew the team needed him to win his quarterfinal match. The stakes had been made painfully clear: for Riverstone to win its first state title, Tyler not only needed to finish in the top three at 130 but also had to advance through the quarterfinals to secure critical championship bracket points. Coach Beau had painstakingly detailed every scenario, scribbling out long equations on the board in the team room. His calculations left no doubt, Tyler's match was a pivotal piece of the puzzle.

The challenge was daunting. Tyler was seeded sixth and matched up against a senior from White Mountain, a former state champion who had already beaten him twice that season. But stepping onto the mat, Tyler felt something different. The doubts and weight of past losses seemed to fade. He was focused, determined. He was on a mission.

The whistle blew, and Tyler burst into action, wrestling with intensity and precision. By the end of the first period, he had dominated, building a commanding 6–1 lead.

At the break, Tyler circled toward the edge of the mat, stealing a glance at Coach Beau. The referee flipped the colored disc into the air, and it landed red.

"Red, your choice," the ref said, turning toward Tyler and Beau. Tyler raised his arms, ready to cross them to signal deferring the choice as usual. But before he could finish the motion, Beau's voice cut through.

"TOP," Beau commanded, his tone firm and deliberate.

Tyler froze and turned to his coach in disbelief. All season the strategy had been to defer in situations like this. The philosophy was straightforward: force the opponent to play to their strength, revealing where they lacked confidence. But now, Beau was changing the script.

"He's panicking," Beau explained, his voice calm but unyielding. "He doesn't know how to wrestle you from behind. Keep the pressure on. This is where all your work pays off."

Swallowing his doubt, Tyler nodded and knelt in the center, covering his opponent as they both froze in position. The whistle blew, and the White Mountain wrestler exploded upward, driving the back of his head into Tyler's face. A flash of white light blurred Tyler's vision, but he reacted instinctively.

Ignoring the pain, Tyler dropped to a single leg, driving forward with relentless energy to capture the far ankle. He pulled his opponent back to the mat, maintaining control. As his opponent scrambled back to his base, Tyler transitioned seamlessly into a spiral ride, circling to elongate his opponent's position and dictate the pace.

This was Tyler's move; the one Beau had drilled into him over countless practices. Beau's voice echoed in his mind: *"Stretch him out, control the motion, then lock in the half. Chest down, head up, and smile for the girls!"*

Tyler executed the sequence with precision, sliding into the half-nelson and driving his opponent flat. The ref dropped to the mat, slapping it decisively.

A pin. And with it, two bonus points for the team.

The gym erupted, the roar of the crowd washing over Tyler like a wave. He rose to his feet, breathless, as the ref raised his hand in victory. Glancing toward the corner, Tyler caught sight of Beau, who was smiling, a rare, genuine grin that spoke volumes.

For a fleeting moment, Tyler felt the weight of the moment. This wasn't just a win for the team. It was for Beau, for all the trust and belief his coach had placed in him. And for the first time, Tyler allowed himself to believe he belonged.

Chapter Nineteen: States

I will not fall,
I will stand tall,
Feels like no one could beat me.
Eminem (feat. Nate Dogg) – "Till I' Collapse"

The gym at Bow High School buzzed with nervous energy, a sound Bryce had come to expect at tournaments. But this was different. This was states. The bleachers were packed with parents, teammates, and alumni, their voices blending into a constant hum that seemed to vibrate through the air. Banners hung high, the colors of rival teams a stark reminder of the competition ahead.

Bryce sat with his teammates beneath the red-and-black Riverstone Wrestling banner, the roaring Saber logo looming above them, a reminder of the program's storied past. Despite his undefeated season, Bryce entered the 165-pound bracket as the 7th seed. Three matches at the weight all year hadn't been enough to earn him respect. He replayed the bracket in his head: his first match against another undefeated wrestler, and if he made it through, a looming final against the top seed, a two-time defending champion who cast a long shadow over the entire weight class.

Bryce leaned forward, elbows resting on his knees, as the doubts crept back in. *Do I even belong here? Did I make the right decision moving up for the team? What if I let everyone down?*

His gaze drifted to his teammates. Some were talking nervously, while others sat with headphones clamped over their ears, locking themselves into the moment. Johnson should've been here. The thought pressed down on Bryce like a weight, heavier than anything he'd lifted in the gym. It felt like the team's entire season rested on his shoulders.

At the top of the bleachers, Tyler stood gripping the railing. Bryce could tell his dad was nervous, even though he worked hard to hide it. This was something Beau loved, delivering the pre-tournament speech with a mix of inspiration and sharp reality checks. Tyler wasn't Beau, but in that moment, Bryce didn't care. He needed his dad to speak, to make it all feel possible.

"You young men have made this an incredible season," Tyler began, his voice steady but carrying the weight of every moment that had brought them here. "You've worked harder than anyone thought possible. You've taken your losses, grown from them, and put yourselves in a position to compete for something bigger than yourselves— a team state championship."

Bryce straightened, the familiar rhythm of Tyler's voice settling the restless energy in his chest.

"But listen to me: being here today, together, sitting here as a team ready to go into battle, you're already champions. It's not about the banner or the medals. It's about what you've built along the way. It's about how you've come together, how you've fought for each other, and how you've never given up."

The gym seemed to quiet as Tyler's words landed. Bryce glanced at Nick beside him. The nervous sophomore fidgeted with his hands, eyes darting nervously toward the mats. Bryce reached over and gave him a quick pat on the shoulder. *You've got this,* he thought, the silent gesture a small reassurance, one he remembered Tyler giving him years ago.

Tyler paused, his voice softening. "Beau used to say wrestling isn't about the medals you win. It's about the journey, the people you share it with, and the lessons you take off the mat. And he was right. Today, I'm proud to stand here with you—not just as your coach, but as someone who's been through this battle before."

Bryce felt the tension in his chest shift, just slightly.

Tyler straightened, his voice rising again. "Now, let's go out there and write the next chapter of Riverstone Wrestling history. Wrestle for yourselves, wrestle for each other, and wrestle for everyone who's ever put on this uniform and left it better than they found it."

The team erupted into their chant, voices rising as one. Bryce joined in, his voice blending with the others. For the first time that morning, the doubts began to fade.

The buzz of early matches filled the gym as the tournament began. Bryce stood near the edge of the Riverstone's bleacher section, watching Nick step onto the mat for his opening match. The kid wrestled like he had nothing to lose, his movements sharp and aggressive. Bryce felt every moment of the match in his chest, silently willing Nick forward. By the final whistle, Nick's arm was raised in victory, the scoreboard reading 10–3.

The Riverstone bleacher section erupted, the cheers breaking through the tension like a wave. Nick turned and grinned at Bryce, as if to say, *Your turn.* Bryce let out a long breath he hadn't realized he was holding, pride and pressure swirling together in his chest. *Nick stepped up. Now it's on me.*

Across the mat, Bryce met Tyler's eyes. His dad gave him a small nod, the kind Bryce had seen a thousand times before. The message was clear: *You've got this.*

"165, Riverstone, red," the ref called.

Bryce jogged to the center of the mat, scooping up the red ankle bands. He slipped them on quickly, the snugness grounding him in the moment. The ritual was familiar, a reminder of every match that had brought him here.

He jogged back to the corner, where Tyler knelt, calm and steady. "This is about your speed, your technique, your conditioning," Tyler said. "You wrestle your match. Control the action. Don't wait. You've got this."

Bryce grinned, a flicker of confidence breaking through the nerves. "Did you see Nick out there? We've got this, Dad. Today, we're getting you that banner...Drill Sergeant!"

Tyler smirked and shook his head at the jab, but Bryce caught the glint of pride in his dad's eyes. He understood what his son was saying, he would go to battle for a team led by Tyler. Because, like Beau, Tyler was the kind of leader you'd follow anywhere.

Turning back to the mat, Bryce stretched his arms out, shaking loose the last of his nerves. Across from him, his opponent loomed, undefeated, confident, and every bit the powerhouse the bracket had promised.

He's bigger. Stronger. Faster, Bryce thought for half a second before he pushed the words away. None of it mattered.

The whistle blew, and Bryce surged forward. The doubts disappeared, replaced by fire and clarity.

Let's rock!

Chapter Twenty - Tyler: Junior Year – States – Blood Round

All my bags are packed

I'm ready to go

John Denver – *"Leaving on a Jet Plane"*

The plan Coach Beau had meticulously laid out on the board was quickly falling into place. Tyler would be facing elimination in the consolation semifinals but stood two wins away from the top three finish the team needed from him to secure the championship banner. Beau worked tirelessly to keep the pressure off his wrestlers, but with each match drawing closer to a critical outcome, even he couldn't shake the growing tension.

The Bennetts sat high in the bleachers, watching the consolation brackets unfold, as they awaited their finals matches that would be held to close out the evening. The Bennet brothers had already pinned their way into the finals, delivering another dominant performance. Now, all eyes were on the nine Riverstone wrestlers still alive in the blood round.

To have any chance at the title, the team needed eight of them to advance. Seven might give them a shot, but it would require an extraordinary number of pins to overcome Pineford—a bitter rival just two towns away. Once part of the same school district, the two programs had become fierce adversaries.

Riverstone's lineup for the consi-semifinals consisted of the 103, 112, 119, 130, 135, 160, 171, 189, and 215 pounds. Getting wrestlers to exceed their limits had always been Coach Beau's specialty. He had an uncanny ability to deliver just the right correction, even when bluntly pointing out mistakes. Instead of making you feel worse, it left you believing he saw something in you that no one else could, and maybe, just maybe, you could see it too. Beau was equal parts Mr. Miyagi, teaching lessons without you realizing it, and "Sneaky Pete," tricking you into believing the impossible was within reach.

"Gentlemen," Beau barked, his voice cutting across the gym. "You've earned your spots in this round. But as Mr. Kane used to say—*Stay hungry. Hungry for your points, hungry for victory, hungry. Period.*"

It was classic Beau: simple but effective. His philosophy was always about forward momentum. If something knocked you off your path, you pivoted and moved forward on a new path towards your objective. That relentless drive was what made Beau such a force on the mat when he sparred. His mission was always clear, keep adjusting, keep driving, and keep moving forward until you reach your goal. In Coach Beau's mind, nothing came from looking back, not in wrestling and not in life.

The mats were cleared, and the consolation semifinals began. Riverstone's 103 and 112-pound wrestlers were up first, competing simultaneously against Pineford opponents. The 103-pounder was key, marked as a consolation finalist on the team board since Monday. Meanwhile, the 112-pounder, a first-year wrestler rapidly developing into a takedown machine, had already surpassed expectations by winning one match. Unfortunately, his next opponent was a tough draw: a lanky kid at least six inches taller, the kind of wrestler people joked had hollow bones. Every time the freshman shot in, the Pineford wrestler snapped his legs away with ease.

Coach Beau, ever animated, paced the mat's edge, barking out instructions. By this point in the season, his voice only required one bag of Halls to remain intact through a tournament day. Yet, out of the corner of his eye, he noticed something unsettling: the plan was starting to unravel.

Earlier in the week, the 103-pounder had asked Beau and Coach Mitchell if he could skip New England's if he qualified at States. He admitted this wasn't his year to win a match, yet alone place, at New England's, so missing the tournament wouldn't feel like a loss. Still, he didn't want to let the team down. His family had planned a vacation to Florida, contingent on him not competing. The coaches had reassured him it was fine to miss New England's, if necessary, but plans shifted. When his parents learned he might qualify, they insisted he finish the season with the team, even if it meant canceling their trip.

Beau was surprised, and impressed, by their commitment. Moments like this reminded him of what he would miss most about this team. For once, he allowed himself to pause and appreciate the journey instead of scanning ahead for potential failures in his grand schemes. But even Beau couldn't have predicted that one of his wrestlers' futures would hinge on a family's vacation plans.

On the mat, the 103-pounder clung to a 5-3 lead with 15 seconds left. The Pineford wrestler popped to his feet, and Coach Mitchell's voice rang out in desperation.

"Hold him down! Ok, you're still good, up by one! You've got this! Stay sharp—SPRAWL! NOOOOO!!!!!"

But in the final seconds, the Pineford wrestler scored a takedown, flipping the match to a devastating 6-5 loss.

Meanwhile, the 112-pounder fought valiantly but fell two points short. Beau turned to console him but stopped cold as he caught a fleeting smile on the 103-pounder's face. It wasn't frustration or sadness. It was something else, a quiet sense of relief that left Beau wondering if, in some small way, the kid was a little too okay with how it had all played out.

Chapter Twenty-One - Nick's Finals

Look, if you had one shot or one opportunity
To seize everything you ever wanted in one moment
Would you capture it or just let it slip?
Eminem – "Lose Yourself"

Nick stood near the edge of the mat, bouncing unevenly, his arms stiff and his breathing shallow. Bryce recognized every nervous twitch, every erratic shift. He'd been there before, every wrestler had. Finals weren't just another match. They were a test where every self-doubt, every mistake from practice, came rushing to the surface under the glaring light.

Bryce moved toward Nick quietly, slipping into the space behind him. He didn't need to say much, Nick didn't need a lecture or more pressure. He just needed something to ground him, to steady his thoughts and bring his body into sync. Bryce leaned in, his voice low and calm.

"We're hungry. Hungry for our team, hungry for ourselves...you're hungry, Nick."

At first, Nick didn't respond, his movements jerky and uncoordinated. But Bryce repeated the words, adding a subtle rhythm to his tone, bouncing slightly as he spoke. Slowly, Nick's stiff posture began to loosen, his bouncing syncing with Bryce's. The tension in his shoulders eased, and his breathing steadied.

Nick turned, his eyes flickering with uncertainty, but there was a spark now, faint but growing. Bryce smiled faintly and placed a hand on Nick's shoulder. "The match is yours before the whistle blows, if you believe it is."

Nick nodded, a smirk breaking through the nerves, and Bryce felt a surge of pride. He wasn't just offering words; he was passing on something deeper. The lessons Tyler had drilled into him, the wisdom Coach Beau had shared, the grounding presence of Snake, all of it was alive in this moment. Bryce felt the weight of that legacy settling on his shoulders, not as a burden, but as a responsibility.

"150, Riverstone, report to the table," the ref called.

Nick jogged toward the table, and Bryce stood back, watching him settle into his stance. For a moment, the gym noise faded, and Bryce's thoughts turned inward. *This isn't just about wrestling. It's about something more. Nick needs this, not just for the team, but for himself.*

As Nick stepped onto the mat, Bryce's focus sharpened. Normally, he'd be off by himself, preparing for his own match, locking into his routine. But not today. Today, Nick needed him more than Bryce needed those extra minutes of solitude.

The whistle blew, and Nick moved cautiously, circling his opponent with tentative steps. Bryce's chest tightened as he saw the nerves creeping back in. "Stay steady! Make him come to you!" he called out, his voice cutting through the chaos.

Nick glanced back at Bryce for just a second, and something shifted. His stance reset, his movements sharper, more deliberate. Bryce exhaled, leaning forward instinctively as if willing Nick to move with more confidence.

The first period ended in a stalemate, counters and escapes leaving neither wrestler in control. Bryce barely noticed the crowd; his entire focus was on Nick's movements, the slight hesitations, that needed correcting.

Come on, Nick. Stay strong, Bryce thought, his fists clenching at his sides. Sweat began to bead on his forehead, and he realized just how much his own energy was feeding into Nick's match.

By the end of the second period, Nick began to find his rhythm. An escape point tied the match, and the crowd erupted, but Bryce's focus never wavered. His voice became a steady anchor, calling out subtle adjustments to keep Nick grounded. Each small victory, an escape here, a defended takedown there, felt like a shared triumph.

This coaching thing is intense, Bryce thought, the corners of his mouth tugging into a small grin. For the first time, he understood the emotions Tyler must have felt all those years, standing just off the mat, able to offer guidance but powerless to aid in the win himself.

The third period ended in a tie, sending the match into overtime. Bryce's heart raced as Nick stepped back onto the mat, his energy visibly waning. His opponent looked fresher, his movements quick and aggressive. Bryce stayed calm, his voice steady and unwavering.

"One more shot, Nick. Your shot. Make it count."

The whistle blew, and Nick lunged forward with everything he had. His opponent countered, twisting to block the attack, but Nick adjusted, shifting his weight and locking his grip. Bryce held his breath as Nick drove forward, the motion fluid and unstoppable. The ref signaled the takedown, and the gym erupted in cheers.

Nick sat on the mat for a moment, his chest heaving, his face a mix of shock and relief. Bryce stepped forward, pulling him into a quick hug as he came off the mat.

"Well," Bryce said with a grin, "I guess now I need to go win my match. Can't let you have all the glory. Hell, maybe I'll steal a little bit of your thunder and stick him."

Nick laughed, the tension from the match finally breaking. Bryce patted him on the back and glanced toward Tyler, who was standing off to the side, watching with quiet pride.

Bryce didn't need words to understand what Tyler was thinking. He wasn't just another wrestler anymore. He was part of something bigger, a light in the darkness, a leader carrying the lessons of those who had come before.

And now, it was his turn to step onto the mat.

Chapter Twenty-two - Tyler: Junior Year — Blood Round Conclusion

Those mountains highs
Those valley lows
I lived them both
Jelly Roll – "Everyone Bleeds"

Tyler watched from a distance as Robby nervously bounced on his toes next to Coach Beau. The young wrestler's agitation was palpable, his energy buzzing like a live wire. Tyler saw Beau take the question like a blow to the gut.

"Shit, Coach, are we done? Like, our chances are fucked, right?" Robby's voice cracked, loud enough that a few heads turned.

Beau's jaw tightened for just a moment, a flicker of something unreadable crossing his face. Then his voice came, sharp and steady. "Enough, Robby. Focus on your match."

It wasn't just an order; it was a lifeline. Tyler recognized it instantly. Beau's words had pulled him back from the edge plenty of times, and now they worked their magic on Robby, who exhaled and nodded, his pace slowing.

Tyler watched Beau with a growing sense of awe. Beau wasn't just coaching moves or strategies; he was coaching belief. For Robby, Beau was a shield, channeling that raw energy into something controlled. For Johnny, he was a quiet guide, pushing gently but firmly. Tyler realized Beau didn't coach them to wrestle; he coached them to see who they could be, even when they couldn't.

The match unfolded like Tyler knew it would, hard-fought and close. Robby's opponent was relentless, every exchange was a test of endurance and will. By the time the third period ended, the match was tied, and overtime loomed.

Tyler watched Beau lean into Robby's ear during the break, his voice calm but urgent. "Your setup, your moves. You lead. Make him go where you want, then get your points."

Tyler saw it then, the flicker of belief in Robby's eyes, that quiet determination Beau always managed to spark. The whistle blew, and Robby surged forward, driving into his opponent with everything he had. But Tyler's heart sank as he saw the shift, the fireman's carry was perfect. Robby was caught. The ref slapped the mat, signaling the pin, and just like that, their shot at the team title was gone.

Robby got up slowly, his head hanging, and walked off the mat in silence. Tyler felt the loss hit him like a punch, but when he looked at Beau, he didn't see despair. Beau's expression was calm, his eyes on Robby. *It's not the outcome. It's the fight.*

Later, after winning his consolation finals match, Tyler approached Beau. The gym felt quieter now, the noise fading into a dull hum as the weight of the season settled over him. Beau turned as Tyler approached, pulling him into a bear hug.

"You've done good, young man," Beau said, his voice warm. "You proved a lot to me, this team, and your mom. You accepted a tough role, and you didn't complain. Well, not too much." His smirk softened the words, and Tyler chuckled despite himself.

"Third in States and heading to New England's at 130 pounds," Beau continued. "I didn't tell you this before, but that's exactly what I did my senior year. It's what brought me back to this sport."

Tyler blinked, surprised. Beau, the man who seemed larger than life, had once stood where he stood now. For the first time, Tyler saw it clearly. Beau didn't coach them to be like him. He coached them to be the best version of themselves.

"You've lost this once, Tyler. Don't lose it again," Beau said, his tone softening. "You have a glow about you when you're around this sport, this mat, and this team. Never forget that."

Later, as the final scores were announced, Riverstone came up just short, taking home the runner-up plaque. Eddie Bennett was named Outstanding Wrestler, securing his fourth championship. His brothers, Johnny and Tommy, joined him in raising their individual banners.

At the last team event, surrounded by Coach Mitchell, Robby, Johnny, and Tyler, Beau addressed them one final time.

"Gentlemen, this is your team now. I know the efforts Eddie, Bagwell, Coach Mitchell and I put in over the last four years are in good hands. I'm excited to see where you take this program. It's your time to lead, time to throw the rope back and be there for each other.

"Remember, the lessons we learned on the mat were never just about wrestling. Reflect on what you've gained: the quiet conversations on the bus rides, the moments of doubt when you leaned on each other, and the times you pushed yourselves further than you thought possible. Those were the moments you grew."

Beau paused, his smirk breaking through. "Too many guys out there don't know how to lean on each other in times of struggle. That's what The Quest was about. That's what Hell Week was about. Torturing you was just a bonus."

The room filled with quiet laughter, the weight, lifting just a little.

"It's about showing you how much you're capable of when you're hungry and when you believe in yourself. Someone gave you a rope to get to this point. What you do with it now, that's up to you. I've shown you all I can show you."

Chapter Twenty-Three – Bryce's Finals

Starin' down a bullet
Let me make my final stand
Jon Bon Jovi – "Blaze of Glory"

Bryce bounced lightly on his feet, headgear in his hand, as the hum of the gym swirled around him. The noise wasn't sharp or overwhelming, it was a steady pulse, a reminder of how many people were watching and waiting for him to deliver. He bounced lightly on his feet, his earbuds drowning out the crowd. But no song could quiet the thoughts racing in his head.

This wasn't just another match. It wasn't even just about the team. This was his chance to rewrite a moment that had haunted him for two years, the semifinal loss to this same opponent, the one who had stolen his shot at a state title. Tonight, it was him or me.

He glanced toward the bleachers, where Nick stood with the rest of the team. Nick's grin was still bright, his confidence buoyed by his earlier win. Bryce couldn't help but smirk. Nick had wrestled his heart out, and now the kid looked like he belonged up there with the greats.

I want that, Bryce thought. *I want to stand up there with them, knowing I earned it.* But it wasn't just about him. If he didn't pin this guy, the team wouldn't have enough points to take home the championship banner. A title wasn't just possible, it was ready to be earned.

Across the gym, Tyler stood with his arms crossed, watching Bryce closely but giving him space. Bryce knew the look on his dad's face: calm and steady, but underneath it was a storm. Tyler might not step onto the mat, but Bryce knew the match mattered to him just as much. For Tyler, wrestling wasn't just a sport. It was legacy, lessons, and moments like this.

Bryce shook his head, breaking away from the weight of expectation. He jogged toward Tyler, pulling out one earbud as he neared. "Dad," he started, his voice low but steady. "Feeling a little hungry. What do you think?"

Tyler's eyes lit with recognition. "I think a good pancake will cure that hunger," he said, his voice calm, but Bryce caught the flicker of pride beneath it.

"Riverstone, red!" the official called, looking toward Bryce. Bryce grabbed the red ankle bands from the scorer's table, snapping them on before moving to the center of the mat. Across from him, his opponent waited, every bit as calm and confident as he remembered. The two-time defending state champion radiated the kind of swagger that came with dominance. Bryce matched it with a quiet intensity of his own.

The whistle blew, and the match was on.

The first minute was a game of cat and mouse. Fakes, counters, quick resets, the dance of two wrestlers testing the other's weaknesses. Bryce's opponent struck first, diving for a double-leg takedown, but Bryce sprawled hard, his legs kicking back as he deflected the attack.

"Reset! Get back to neutral!" Tyler's voice cut through the chaos.

Bryce felt the familiar tug of his dad's words, grounding him. This wasn't just about counters and moves. This was about making his opponent think he was a step ahead, only to pull the rug out from under him.

Let him think he's got it, Bryce thought, his mind racing. *Let him think I'm just holding on.*

As the first period ticked down, Bryce stayed disciplined, baiting his opponent with small openings. The second period started, and the dynamic shifted. His opponent lunged for a single leg, driving forward with power. Bryce deflected again, this time twisting toward the edge of the mat.

"Now!" Tyler's voice rang out, and Bryce knew it was time.

As his opponent overcommitted, Bryce swung his left arm into a Whizzer, locking it in tight and driving his opponent's head toward the mat. His heart pounded, the moment crystallizing in his mind.

This is it. He's mine.

With a sudden twist, Bryce transitioned. His right arm swung around, locking the head, and he drove forward with everything he had. The pancake hit clean, his opponent's shoulders slammed into the mat, and Bryce pressed down, feeling the resistance give way.

The ref dropped, checking the shoulders. Bryce held his breath, his muscles straining, the world narrowing to this single moment.

The whistle blew. Pin.

For a second, the gym was silent, as if no one could believe what had just happened. Then the crowd erupted, the roar washing over Bryce like a tidal wave. He rolled off his opponent and shot to his feet, his arms raised high.

I did it. We did it.

He turned toward the Riverstone section of the bleachers, where his teammates were already rushing toward him. Nick was the first to reach him, throwing his arms around Bryce with a grin so wide it looked like his face might split.

"We did it," Bryce said, his voice rough with emotion. "All of us."

The rest of the team swarmed around him, their voices a chaotic mix of cheers and shouts. Bryce glanced back at his dad, who stood a few feet away, his face unreadable for a moment. Then Tyler smiled, a rare, genuine smile that spoke volumes. Bryce knew what it meant.

This wasn't just a win. It was Bryce stepping into his role, not just as a champion, but as a leader.

As the team lifted him onto their shoulders, Bryce let himself soak in the moment. The lights, the cheers, the banner waiting to be raised, it wasn't just for him. It was for every practice, every loss, every time they'd pushed each other to be better.

He wasn't hungry anymore. He was satisfied.

For now.

Chapter Twenty-Four - Full Circle

When you get where you're going don't forget to turb back around

And help the next one in line

Tim McGraw – "Humble And Kind"

Hours later, after the team had returned from the tournament, Tyler reflected in the same spot where he stood months ago, carrying the weight of broken memories and unfulfilled promises. The banners above the mat swayed gently in the draft, their golden letters catching the dim light. Tyler stood alone in the darkness, staring at the space where Bryce, Nick, and the team would raise their banners in a few months.

He closed his eyes, breathing in the silence. This place, which had once smelled of regret, now carried something else, hope. Tyler could feel it in the air, see it in the way Bryce lifted his teammates, and hear it in the echoes of their laughter, still faintly alive in the gym's empty corners.

He thought of Beau, of Snake, and of the long line of lessons passed down from coach to wrestler, from mentor to leader. Each of them had been a light for someone, guiding them through the darkness. Tyler's mind drifted to something Beau had told him long ago: *"It's not just about winning, it's about what you leave behind. Reach back to help those who come after you, and they'll climb higher than you ever did."*

He opened his eyes and glanced up at the banners, their frayed edges whispering memories of the past. This time, though, he didn't see a gutted program or a legacy in ruins. He saw a future, a bright one, carried by Bryce and Nick and the team they had built together.

Robby and Beau had been right. Tyler needed to find his own light again. The weight he had carried wasn't just guilt or regret, it was the loss of his own belief in what wrestling, what *this program*, had once given him. But tonight, standing in this gym, Tyler saw it again. Not just in himself, but in Bryce, who was becoming a gift to the world, a light for others, just as Beau had been for Tyler, and Snake for Beau.

Tyler smiled, a single tear slipping down his cheek. This time, there was no shame in it, no anger. Beau's words echoed in his mind, as clear and steady as if he were standing beside him: *"Now is a fine time to cry. Those aren't tears of darkness…they are of light."*

He turned toward the door, glancing one last time at the banners and the mat below them. The gym didn't feel like a place of regret anymore. It felt like home.

Walking out of the gym, Tyler felt a sense of peace he hadn't known in years. The team, the legacy, the rope, they were in good hands. Bryce had the light now, and Tyler had rediscovered his own.

Epilogue

When you make it out the shadows, you wanna
be a light
Every day's a blessin' when you shouldn't be alive
Jelly Roll - "Smile So Much"

Mikey (Coach Beau) sat in his usual spot at the kitchen table, in the small, raised cape overlooking Governors Lake. It was the seat that let him keep his back to the wall, a habit born from years of living on edge. From this spot, he could see the past as clearly as the rock outside, a symbol of stability that carried generations of memories. But today, as he tried to write his father's eulogy, the rock was no anchor. Instead, it felt like a weight dragging him into the depths of his pain.

"Have a great trip grandma, I love you and will see you in the spring. I'll take care of the house and your car this winter," the last words Mikey said to his grandmother, 5 in the morning as she sat where Mikey sat now. His grandfather had died that previous Easter, losing his battle to cancer, it had been decided that it was best if Mikey, 24, moved in to look over everything. It wasn't ideal, the house, at the time, was set up as a raised ranch, with a single bedroom and bathroom, so Mikey lived on a futon in the basement.

Mikey had gotten his grandmother, on his mom's side, a chauffeured ride to Logan Airport so she could head to Florida for the winter. Less than four months later, Mikey was in a hospital room at CMC in Manchester saying goodbye as she lost her battle to pancreatic cancer, which her having hidden from all how sick she was, longing to join Mikey's Grandfather in heaven.

"I think it's time for you to buy a house", Mikey's mom had said to him, two months after the funeral. Eight weeks later, Mikey was sitting at a closing table, looking at a stack of documents that sent even his keen financial and business mind spinning.

The spot at the table had originally been Mikey's grandfather's, a place where he could eat and watch football at the same time, a habit Mikey quickly adopted. From that spot Mikey could see where, under the window overlooking the rock that symbolized Mikey's foundation, his grandfather's battle with cancer came to an end.

That rock held so much history. It was where Mikey's parents first met during a warm July summer. His dad, then a 14-year-old boy, had water-skied in, spraying the 13-year-old blonde girl with a playful mist as he came to a sharp stop. In that instant, his father's smile and eyes captured her attention, and from that moment, their lives moved forward together through highs and lows.

Mikey was 23 when his grandfather passed, extinguishing a light that had shielded and guided him, as well as many others. It wasn't until that light went dark that Mikey began to truly see what had shaped him. For most, such realizations might not seem unusual. For Mikey, however, clarity always seemed to come during his lowest moments, where understanding often arrived alongside pain.

Shortly after purchasing the house, Mikey was in that spot to write his Papa's eulogy. Ironically, where he had been sitting when he noticed the lights on after midnight at Grammie and Papa's cabin across the lake, where Mikey's dad had spent his summer, when he got home that night. He had visited with his grandparents earlier in the day, sitting for an hour just enjoying the late July air before heading to see Rosalyn as she got off work.

Mikey had met Rosalyn earlier that month, but didn't really realize how much of a hold she had on him until he was walking around that July 23, 1998 night in Vegas, having just witnessed, as much as a non-Mormon can witness a Mormon wedding, his best friend Caleb getting married in St. George, UT that morning. Mikey felt so proud standing in the receiving line next to Caleb and Melanie, his new bride, as the whole community of Kanab, UT came to give their congratulations to the young newlyweds. Walking alone that night, all Mikey wanted was to be holding the hand of the woman who turned Mikey's eye like no other ever had. Rosalyn had appeared before Mikey as if she had dropped from heaven, standing on his front lawn that July 4, 1998. He looked down at her from the deck, where he cockily stood wrapped in just a towel, and for the first time, he truly saw the real woman behind that welcoming smile.

"We need a happy occasion, like a wedding", Mikey's mom would say to Rosalyn at Papa's funeral. Mikey turning red as he had only been with Rosalyn for a couple of weeks at the time. Sure, within eight days of their first kiss, Mikey and Rosalyn were admitting that the connection between them was love, but marriage was not anything to discuss at that moment!

However, Mikey's mom had been right, as Mikey and Rosalyn were married July 23, 1999, on Caleb and Melanie's first anniversary. Mikey and Rosalyn had the dee-jay play a special song for their occasion. A few years after Mikey and Rosalyn had finished having children, Grammie had passed, finally succumbing to the effects of a stroke suffered two years earlier. Mikey was sitting blocked when Rosalyn handed him a poem, "The Dash" by Linda Ellis. Mikey rolled his eyes in disgust, something that Rosalyn had learned to ignored as the frequency of the eye rolls was only outnumbered by Michael's sarcasm, or more often, his self-deprecation.

"I was struggling to write this eulogy", standing again at the very same podium where he had delivered what had been a wonderfully crafted tribute to his Papa, his first real showing of his writing and depth of human understanding, *"my lovely wife Rosalyn handed me a poem, "The Dash" and*

said I might find it helpful. I looked, gave her my dismissive 'yeah right' Beaudet family eye roll, and just shook my head. Well, once again, she knew where I needed to be pointed. The dash explains how on one's tombstone, it is not the numbers on either side of the dash, but the time within the dash, when one lives, and experiences so much, and that when someone shares those experiences with others, that is when life has meaning." As always, Mikey couldn't hear his own words, never realizing what others might have learned from him and all he has shared.

So, Mikey decided to try to use the internet for some guidance on how to honor his dad. How does he turn such darkness, there is no other way to look at suicide, Mikey knowing this firsthand having wondered if his eternal darkness was the best answer for all those he loved. All of those who he knew, he was risking whenever he turned away from the light of others and decided he would go it alone. Mikey felt most secure, alone playing in his room, unable to disappoint anyone and free from the feeling of needing to carry the burden. A trait you learn as a latchkey only child, who took on a role of independence at too young of an age.

"I'm trying to write a tribute to one of the smartest people I've ever known, someone who was so shaped by experiences, learning from doing over sitting being lectured. Read, interpret, and go, that was how I was taught, the answers are all there, you just need to read and apply," he said to himself as he tried searching for quote on intelligence, knowledge, etc.

"Wisdom is the knowledge which sees the depth of things, which penetrates to the roots," a thought put forward by Paul Tillich stop Mikey for a moment. Something about that seemed too shallow, while he agreed with most of it, something just bugged him about it. The phrase seemed to be internalized, whereas Mikey felt knowledge is something that is leant to you.

"Bullshit. Being wise isn't about how far someone's gone—it's about what they've learned along the way. That's what shapes the lens that filters everything they see. Wisdom? It's sharing that lens, helping others find their path, and protecting them from the darkness." Mikey proclaimed.

But how could Mikey really do this, he knew what would happen, it was why he avoided writing. He knew how the darkness would hit him. Was he strong enough to turn and face it?

"You know what you need to do, right?" the voice, the ever-internal AI within Mikey, Snake was again in his mind.

"If I do, I'm going to cry and your boys don't cry," was the answer that left Mikey feeling justified. Until he thought about that day, standing over Swanny's casket when Snake placed his heavy hand on Mikey's shoulder and said:

"Sometimes, you can't do anything but cry…to flush away the darkness. But don't let the crying be the end. When

the tears stop, that's when you need to bring the light back in. That how you fight son. That's how you find you strength."

And with that thought, Mikey knew what he had to do. He closed out of his web search and opened Microsoft Word and started typing. Pushing through the darkness to find the light in life's lessons and challenges.

Go back to where the story began in Snake's Boys, where Snake's unwavering belief in the power of resilience and mentorship shapes the next generation, beginning with a young boy who didn't yet know the weight of his own potential.

Snake's Boys

Version 2024.12.14
by
Peter Bergeron

Snake's Boys - Chapter 1 Mikey – Boys Club Van

Well, there's a little boy waiting
At the counter of the corner shop
He's been waiting down there, waiting half the day
They never ever see him from the top
Moving Pictures – "What About Me"

"Boys' club pickup to zone five," crackled through the antique speaker in Mrs. Doucett's dimly lit second-grade classroom at North Side Elementary. The distorted voice barely carried over the shuffle of the few remaining stragglers, children lingering at their desks or waiting noisily by the door for the bus. Most of the kids were especially rambunctious this time of year, filled with anticipation for the upcoming Christmas break.

At the back of the room, Mikey sat alone, pencil in hand, scribbling furiously on a piece of paper. The solitude suited him, and Mrs. Doucett watching from her desk, found the sight familiar. Over the past few months, she had observed Mikey often seeming miles away from the world around him. Content in his own corner, he allowed the chatter of others to fade into the background. Mikey did not naturally gravitate toward conversations; he seemed most at ease adrift in his own thoughts.

"Mikey, you are going to miss your ride to the boys' club." Mrs. Doucett called out to the quiet boy.

"Ok, Mrs. D, thank you, I'll see you tomorrow," he sheepishly stated, as he swung his oversized backpack over one shoulder, the weight landing uncomfortably on his back.

"Have fun Mikey," the kind teacher said.

"Yeah...ok...", and with that Mikey shuffled into the hallway.

His shuffle turned into hurried steps as he rounded the corner toward Zone Five. His parents' lax attention to drop off times had taught him early that being left behind came with its own kind of loneliness. He still remembered the sting of the bus pulling away without him, the laughter of other kids as he sat on the curb. Not today, Mikey thought.

Lost in his thoughts, Mikey almost barreled into Kenny, who himself was walking to the pick-up area, ready to jump on bus 317. Mrs. G, the driver of bus 317, lived in the same neighborhood as Kenny and Mikey. With her youngest son being friends with Kenny's older brother, they had found themselves over at Mrs. G's house a few times during the summer. She made some of the most amazing cucumber sandwiches, that helped quench the thirst of a pack of hungry boys who had spent the day chasing frogs in the river that fed Arlington Pond.

"Whoa there, Mikey," Kenny said, stepping aside with a grin. "Where's the fire?"

"Sorry Kenny," Mikey mumbled, trying to sidestep and keep moving.

Kenny matched his pace, walking beside him. "Relax, you're not gonna miss that old rust bucket. It's sooo broken down; I'm surprised it gets out of the parking lot. You ever notice how it leans to one side, like it's about to tip over?"

Mikey glanced at him, his lips twitching at the mental image Kenny painted.

"Bet you ten bucks it'll fall apart on the way back today," Kenny added, nudging Mikey with his elbow. "The driver'll probably have to duct-tape the doors shut to keep us all inside."

That did it. Mikey let out a short laugh, and Kenny grinned like he'd just won a prize.

"There it is!" Kenny said. "I knew you had a laugh in there somewhere. Thought I was gonna have to tickle it out of you."

Mikey shook his head, the corners of his mouth still curved upward. "The van's not that bad."

"Oh, it's worse," Kenny said dramatically, throwing his arm out as if mimicking the van lurching side to side. "But hey, we get where we're going. Barely."

They reached the door to the pick-up zone, where the infamous blue van was idling, puffing out clouds of white exhaust. Kenny clapped Mikey on the back.

"Go on, little bro," he said, giving him a playful push. "Don't let 'em take off without you. I'll see you inside."

Mikey hesitated for a moment, looking back at Kenny. "Thanks," he said quietly.

Kenny shrugged. "What are brothers for?"

As Mikey walked over to Zone 5, he could see the blue broke-down Boys' Club van, with the usual group of misfits who, like Mikey, had no one to go home to after school. For the past year and a half, every day after school, Mikey would get onto the van and sit quietly in the corner, never feeling like he fit in, as his life was not like the others around him.

Most kids spent their times with their siblings and surrounded by childish laughter. Or spend time playing team sports, but Mikey on the other hand spent the majority of his time as the only kid amongst adults, being an only child of young parents, whose friends had not started their own families yet. Mikey learned quickly to be seen, but not heard, which made him the perfect target for those kids who were looking to escape the shame they felt for their own upbringings. It was why Mikey drifted away from things that created extra interactions with kids.

"Man, Mikey, you must've been one ugly baby if your momma never wanted another one!", came from the back of the van as one of the sixth graders started in early on the meek second grader. Mikey tried to ignore it, but it was just the start of a typical afternoon for him. Around other kids, he just felt like an outcast, except for Kenny, a kid a grade ahead of Mikey, who lived less than a half mile from Mikey, and they had met within a day of Mikey's family moving to Salem four years ago.

Kenny's life was quite different than Mikey, living with his single mother, his three brothers, his sister, and his grandmother. Like Mikey, Kenny and his siblings barely saw their mom, and Mikey was quickly adopted as the youngest family member of the Romanski family. Even still, Mikey's mom insisted that he go to the boys' club after school, as she wasn't always sure when they would get home. If a customer was coming for a pickup that evening, then getting the work done took priority over everything else, as was the way in the Beaudet family. Kenny made Mikey feel like he actually wasn't an only child, around Kenny he felt like he had a brother.

The van slowly made its way into the Boys' Club parking lot. Several of the older kids took the chance to bounce their backpacks and lunchboxes off Mikey as they got off the van. Every hit causing the group of misfits to laugh a little bit louder, until finally the van driver notices what is happening. Although given that it is a near daily event, it is surprising how long it takes for him to get involved. "Hey, knock it off guys, this is not how we are supposed to treat the other members of the club!" The announcement falls on deaf ears as the boys ran into the club.

"You ok Mikey?"

"Sure, Mr. M., it's no big deal…I'm fine, thank you", was all that the ever quiet 8-year-old would answer as he shuffled off into the club. A large figure Mikey hadn't seen before was holding the door open for as Mikey as he walked up the slight ramp to the club.

"How are you doing on this bright, crisp winter day?" the stranger asked. As Mikey stepped nearer, the man seemed to grow, his enormous frame balanced by a steady, calm voice that somehow felt even larger, filling the space around them.

"Ummm, I'm good…thanks…" and with that little Mikey ran into the club. As he ran away, Mikey kept thinking about the voice of the large man. Something about the man's voice felt different—steady, calm, like it wasn't asking anything of him. Mikey couldn't remember ever feeling that safe before. Maybe he never had. It was strange, but for a moment, it made the weight he always carried feel a little lighter. At the moment, Mikey actually found himself bouncing a little as he headed down the hall.

"That kid, I don't know Snake," stated Mr. McGuire as he approached Snake at the door, "that's a shy kid. He's a damn target and he just, I don't know, he just…".

"That boy's lost, McGuire. But there's a spark in him – I can see it," Snake said as they walked inside. "We just have to help him find it".

Get ready for the next chapter in this journey. Snake's Boys will take you deeper into the lessons, the struggles, and the victories that shaped us all.

About the Author
Meet Peter S. Bergeron

Peter Bergeron is a writer, organizational leader, and thinker who thrives at the intersection of creativity, strategy, and leadership. With a career spanning executive roles in finance and operations,

Peter combines practical experience with an academic lens to craft compelling narratives that educate, inspire, and challenge conventional thinking.

Peter's nonfiction work explores leadership, organizational development, small business dynamics, and family business succession, offering readers actionable insights drawn from real-world experience and cutting-edge theories. His writing bridges the gap between strategy and humanity, weaving together concepts like transformational leadership, adaptability, and resilience into engaging and thought-provoking articles. On the creative side, Peter's fiction delves into the complexities of human relationships, leadership struggles, and the delicate balance between ambition and integrity. His stories are driven by relatable characters navigating ethical dilemmas and personal growth, with song lyrics from country music artists often setting the tone for his chapters, reflecting his love of storytelling through music.

In addition to his professional and creative pursuits, Peter is a doctoral student specializing in leadership and organizational development, further deepening his understanding of how people and systems thrive under pressure. His academic work complements his writing, blending research-backed frameworks with practical applications to empower readers and leaders alike. When he's not writing or shaping business strategies, Peter enjoys spending time with his wife, Caroline, sharing their love of motorcycles, boats, and staying fit. Together, they chase endless summers, snow birding between Raymond, NH, and Cape Coral, FL, with their dog by their side. He treasures time spent with his kids, family, and friends and is an avid fan of college wrestling and country music. These passions often find their way into his work, with music and personal reflections infusing his stories with authenticity and heart.

Peter's work is a testament to his belief that storytelling—whether through fiction or nonfiction—is the ultimate tool for connection, growth, and change. Explore his articles, stories, and insights to discover how his words can spark transformation, both in life and in business.